I0822589

The Princess
or
The I Love Paris Ball

A Reminiscence by
Juliette du Tyrac de Marcellus

The Princess
or
The I Love Paris Ball

A Reminiscence by
Juliette du Tyrac de Marcellus

Lake Trail Fiction

Academica Press
Washington~London

Library of Congress Cataloging-in-Publication Data

Names: du Tyrac de Marcellus, Juliette. (author)
Title: The princess, or the i love paris ball | Juliette du Tyrac de Marcellus
Description: Washington : Academica Press, 2022.
Identifiers: LCCN 2022931437 | ISBN 9781680538625 (hardcover) | 9781680538632 (paperback) | 9781680538649 (e-book)

This is a work of fiction. Names, characters, business, events and incidents are the products of the author's imagination. Any resemblance to actual persons, living or dead, or actual events is purely coincidental.

Contents

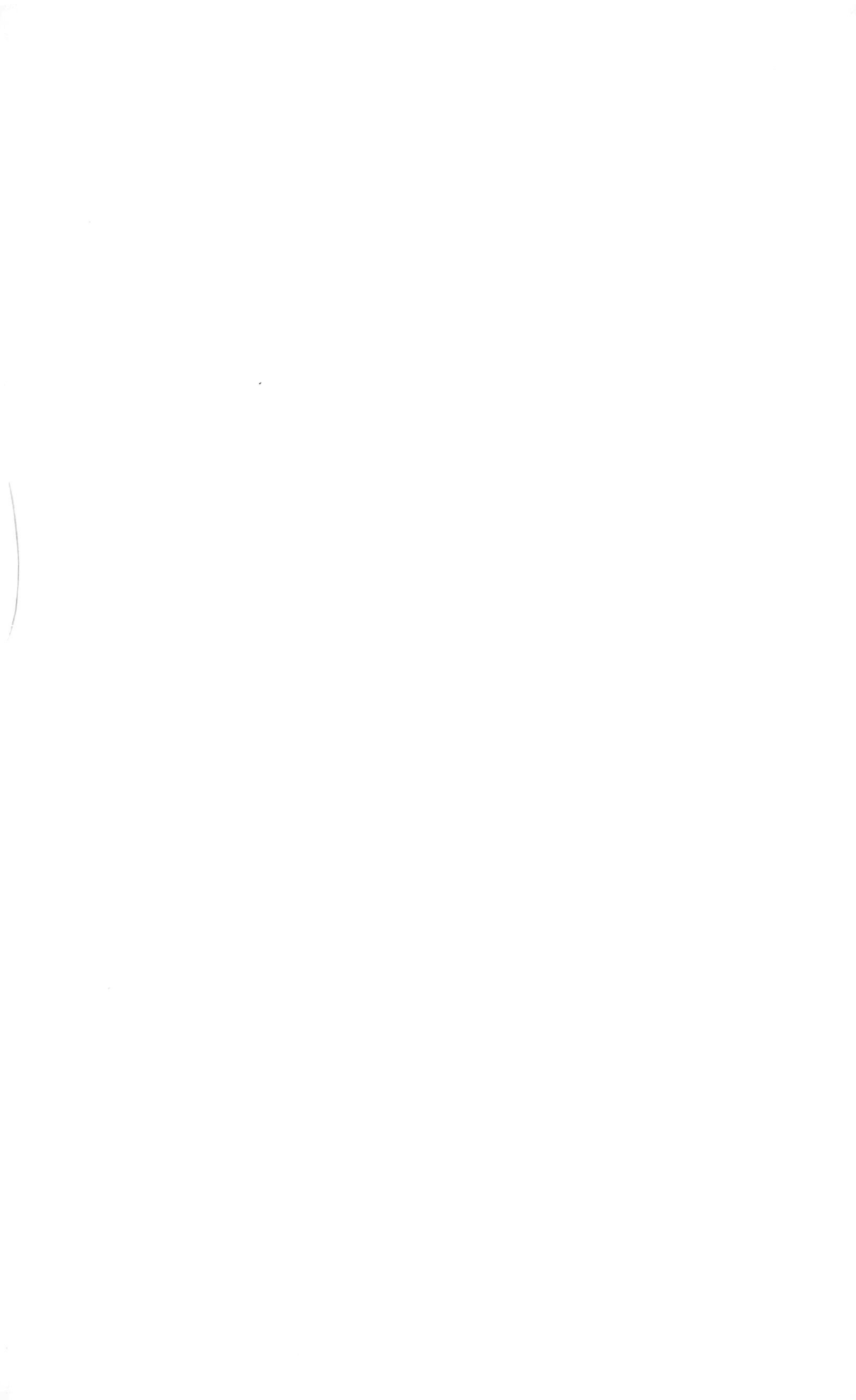

Chapter 1

When you see her today the Princess is pictured, smiling slightly, on the cover of magazines. On inside pages she is seen looking concerned at state funerals, flooded villages, Ascot and nuclear power plants. She politely refuses to give tips on dieting or dress; she grants few interviews. A rose has been named for her.

Her marriage into a reigning royal house took place in a national cathedral on a hazy autumnal day in the presence of three crowned heads and five television cameras. It was the event of the season.

That was the year of the now legendary first and last I Love Paris Ball. It was the year that Hollywood producer/director Sam Kraznik was sued by a noted French novelist for unwarranted distortions of his novel, *Les Cousines*. This notoriously salacious film – made on location in a French château – caused a cinematographic scandal, but, nevertheless, won the International Directors award in Cannes.

But the way in which these three events came about has never been generally understood – certainly not by the Dowager Queen Helen of Kravonia, who discussed the wedding with intimates over coffee and Canasta in Cascais that autumn, nor by the Dowager Duchesse de Ruissy, Chairman of the I Love Paris Ball, both of whom thought they knew. Nor was it understood by those who were responsible for the film, released under the title *By Kiss and By Kin.*

The fact is that the catalyst for bringing about these three memorable events, events that season memorable, as none other than Clarky Finch – listed annually in the Social Register as Clarkson Beard Finch, III of Westhampton and Park Avenue – and Clarky is not someone one would credit with bringing anything about.

It all happened long ago, in the sixties, an era that seems not only distant but almost forgotten, when Clarky Finch stood on his left leg in Paris's Place Vendôme, close to the entrance of the Ritz hotel, while his right foot – lightly shod in an Italian hand-made shoe – gently ground out the stub of his Gauloise cigarette.

Smoking Gauloise cigarettes was the only piece of French culture Clarky had assimilated during all the trips he had made to France. He felt that French cigarettes were somehow manlier than Americans ones, and was slightly disappointed when he was told they were actually less dangerous.

He stood there on the *pavé du roi* and tried to think of an answer to his friend's remark. His friend, Alex Feldenstein, scion of the Feldensteins of the Feldenstein galleries of Paris and New York, had said that with a car like his he could pick up anything.

Clarkson Beard Finch would have liked to have picked up anything; in fact, he had probably had that in mind when he had chosen the car, but when the time came he never found it easy. The girl's eyes frightened him and they always took his money. In the end he didn't say anything, he just smiled.

"Tina Kraznik's in town," said Alex; Alex was always saying who is in town.

"Tina who?"

"Don't you know Tina Kraznik?"

"Oh, sure," Clarky said, and smiled again. The last time Clarky had – in fact the only time – he had ever seen Tina Kraznik was at a gallery party in New York, no doubt at the Feldensteins, when she had come in with some photographer from *Talk* magazine. Clarky always smiles when he doesn't know what to say.

"She's at the Hotel George V, room 222."

"Is that right?"

"Why not call her?"

"I don't actually know her that well."

As both boys were still in their early twenties they were justifiably proud of being able to say they new someone who had nearly been named Model of the Year by *Fashion* magazine; someone who had been the chosen model for the designer Pietro Calamagni for an entire season – her picture everywhere – before marrying a movie mogul and disappearing into Hollywood.

Alex added, "Do you know Olivia Bryce-Smith?"

"No."

"Neither do I. Model. British. Supposed to be a hot number. Want me to fix you up?"

Clarky did not want to be fixed up. He preferred to look around before he spent any money.

This memory of Clarky Finch standing there in the Ritz doorway with Alex came to me as I went through old files the other day and remembered that long-ago season of the I Love Paris Ball, the Royal wedding and the scandalous black-listed movie all inexplicably tied together with Clarky Finch and his languid appearance at the Ritz that afternoon.

At that time I had graduated to the position of society editor at *This is It* magazine. My job chiefly consisted of writing my column *Where Are They Now?*, in which I followed the activities of those who made up a largely imaginary world that was known as High Society.

Clarky was a familiar figure to those of us who clocked the doings of the younger social set at home in the States, so I was not surprised to see him there, standing with his friend at the entrance of the hotel.

It was an era when sons of the *Social Register*, like Clarky, roamed through social gatherings from Southampton to Palm Beach, always welcome and usually late. And one must bear in mind that at that time everyone knew what one meant by High Society – or The International Set – and who was in it. Everyone knew that this world was inhabited by the in-crowd within which were to be found a species known as playboys. The playboy could be seen standing around everywhere that mattered, elegantly holding gold cigarette lighters.

It was a society made up of names made famous by gossip columnists. During that era the great gossip merchants were celebrities in their own right, generously rewarded by the owners of the most fashionable restaurants for mentioning those who frequented them. And those restaurants were reigned over by Maître D's who could make or break you according to what table they chose to give you.

These columnists had created an entire stock company of familiar characters, of whom even Clarky was one. They recorded what they wore, where they went and who they married. These became household names to the many readers of the press; they were recorded as being seen in all the right places with all the right people: fashionable hostesses, polo players, ex-movie stars, and, of course, plain old millionaires.

The columnists lent celebrity to all these, as they tracked their movements from Newport and Southampton to the great European spas and hotels, such as the one I found myself in that day.

And this was not all; this world they documented was seeded with minor royalty who lit up the pages of our magazines.

There were half a dozen European royal families from nations – now democratic or socialist – which had retained their figurehead monarchs; they were for use chiefly in ceremonies which would encourage tourism. They were following the timeless example of Great Britain, and, of course, Monaco. These small monarchies were survivors of two world wars and had narrowly escaped being enveloped by the USSR in 1945. They married each other or into show business; there were even despots from the Middle East doing this.

It is all different nowadays when royals and near royals prefer to be seen doing the dishes and changing their babies' nappies; in those days, in the post war days, they replayed the aura of turn-of-the-century courts, and they gave a special sparkle to our job in the professional gossip world.

That afternoon when I saw Clarky Finch, I was at the Ritz on assignment for *This Is It.* I was to get a picture of one of the debs who had come from New York to be part of the I Love Paris Ball.

It had all started in New York with a meeting called by Sidney B. Schlatz, chairman of Bilco Oil. Mr. Schlatz was not a man known for the elegance of his manners, or the culture of his mind, but he was known as a man who had made many millions for himself and his company – a company which had come to challenge the great oil companies from the Middle East to Texas. His wife and he had not made it into the Social Register, however their daughter, Patty, was now nineteen, a pleasant girl, but neither a great beauty nor distinguished by scholarship.

The question that now arose for the Schlatz family was how to launch Patty into society: without a lot of social credits how were they going to make her Deb of the Year?

The problem did not seem to be insurmountable to them. Sidney Schlatz and his wife had never found themselves unable to pay for what they wanted; they now determined to organize something that would outrank all the deb parties being given in New York and Long Island. As for these gala affairs, given for girls whose families had arrived first, she had only been invited to a few and to others not at all.

Having been to Paris a number of times for meetings with oil executives, Mr. Schlatz decided that what he wanted for his daughter was a big international ball. He (and Bilco Oil) were prepared to underwrite whatever it took. He decided that the resultant publicity would be good for his company as well, and he would call it the I Love Paris Ball.

As society editor at *This Is It*, I was convened to the first planning meeting for this. We had been sent a release concerning the plan by the staff at Bilco Oil; of course the business side of the magazine saw advertising revenue from the oil company as a reward for ample coverage.

The meeting was held in the New York office of Bilco, where I found myself together with the representatives of the French Alliance for Arts and Culture and a secretary from the French Embassy.

Schlatz opened the meeting saying he was planning to underwrite an event which would bring the French and Americans closer together on a society footing. He would be creating a committee to facilitate this in Paris; the committee would suggest where the ball should be held and the people to be invited. He wanted French High Society.

At this point both the woman from the Alliance for Arts and Culture and the one from the Embassy looked troubled. The woman from the Alliance made an effort to explain the makeup and divisions of French society.

For instance, the divide that existed between modern moneyed French and the impecunious world of the old French names was a very difficult thing to explain to someone to whom Paris was only a place of restaurants, beautiful boulevards and museums you didn't actually visit.

How could she explain the gulf that existed between what was known as "Old France" and this contemporary world? I saw them hesitate: the one from Arts and Culture said, "The trouble is, Mr. Schlatz, French society doesn't work the way it does here. You can't say there is High Society in the same way."

"What d'you mean no High Society?" asked Schlatz.

"Well it just doesn't work the same way," she said. "French society is divided."

"Well, we want the best" he said." Can't you help us get some counts and countesses along?"

The ladies continued to look troubled. Even if a ball in Paris could be organized the question remained as to who would come, as girls did not come out in France in the same way. In fact, did French girls come out in France at all?

"You see, Mr. Schlatz," the daughters of the aristocracy don't come out the same way as they do in America. They get to know each other at private parties: they call them "*rallies*," and the other girls go straight to skiing and St. Tropez without bothering to come out. And, well, the trouble is, Mr. Schlatz, that the counts and countesses don't have any money. And it's hard to get to know them."

"Don't tell me that," said Schlatz. "I have a dook on my payroll in Paris.

Now in a way this was true: the Duke in question, Hervé Hubert Marie Jean, Comte de Beauvais, Duke de Ruissy – honorary director for public relations with Bilco Oil in Paris – did exist.

This duke was an elegant well-known figure, the world's idea of a French aristocrat – partly because he looked so English. His profile was more moderate than is usually seen in the best families of France; he was well tailored and slightly greying at the temples. The French were quite proud of him as long as they could continue to be convinced that he was ruined. What needed explaining to someone like Mr. Schlatz, who was short on European history, were the revolutions of 1793 and 1848, the forced division of property between heirs of an estate, according to the Napoleonic Code, to say nothing of the inheritance taxes, both of which had successively bankrupted the land-owning families of France throughout the last one hundred and fifty years.

The duke in this case was evidence of a glorious past, like the historic house he still lived in – an ancient building which many paid a few francs to walk through (in the 60s they were still using francs, of course). And he had found a way to capitalize financially on his looks and his situation in the interest of hanging on to his home, the château de Ruissy, for one more generation. In this endeavour he had allowed himself to become the public relations representative of several American companies in France. These were concerns that paid generous directorship fees as Bilco Oil did, and as did the Interlinear Metals Corporation of Minnesota and a few others. He had opened his three country estates to the general public and made a number of trips to the British Isles to see how they managed to make Stately Homes pay.

What many visitors to France do not realize is that no estate can be preserved without extraordinary measures due to the Napoleonic code that requires all assets be divided equally between heirs. This was established in order to break up the estates, the forests, the vineyards, which it had effectively done.

An estate such as the Château de Ruissy was therefore more of an albatross around the neck of its owner, as the properties that had supported it had long since been divided away among cousins. The duke had made something by commercializing his château within the tourist industry, and had also found American firms who appreciated his representation. And having made something of a success of this, the French government had named him to head the Association for the Preservation of Historic Monuments, which was his chief interest – other, of course, than preserving his own château, famous for its picturesque grandeur. He often said to visiting American businessmen that he hoped the first historic monuments the government preserved was himself; he would say this in his charming accent.

His wife, Henriette, was not above helping him entertain visiting American executives. She understood that if being a Duke and Duchess were to become a minor industry, it would be better supported by American dollars.

Finally, Mr. Schlatz closed the meeting by saying he would contact the dook through the Paris office; there was no reason for the dook not to help put together a committee of French High Society for the Ball.

In fact, of course, this would suit Hervé de Ruissy, whose mother, the dowager duchess, and he were in never-ending search for not just a way to keep the château in good order, but to keep it at all.

"I'll tell you what," said Schlatz, "we will make the ball benefit historic houses in France, the dook will take care of that."

Meanwhile his executive secretary said, making a note on her pad, that she would get in touch with Charlotte Schlemmer, who would be far more helpful in this regard.

But at that time I was not aware who Mrs. Schlemmer was or the role she was to play.

It was in this way that the I Love Paris Ball began to come into a precarious existence under the chairmanship of the Dowager Duchesse de Ruissy and underwritten by Bilco Oil. Meanwhile a number of parents, several connected to the oil company, were convinced that their daughters would meet International society if they made up the group to be presented at the I Love Paris ball.

At a second planning meeting the question of attracting some French debs had to be faced. The ball had to at least have the semblance of being international. Someone suggested it might help if they changed the name from the I Love Paris Ball to The Lafayette Friendship Ball, but Mr. Schlatz stuck with his original idea, saying very sensibly that there was that great tune that the band could play as a theme to the party.

The woman from the Alliance of Arts and Culture made a tentative suggestion: she said that M. and Mme. de la Rocque, members of the Alliance, often came to their meetings; he was professor of finance and economy at New York College of Business – more importantly, Professor de la Rocque was understood by those in the know to be a

"Count," and whose name was actually de la Rocque Tourbonnière, though they shortened it in the United States. At the university he was usually referred to as "Prof. Roc." His wife was a quiet, pleasant American from Boston, she said, and they had two daughters – one was applying to law school, but the younger one was what one could call a debutante.

Someone quite timidly suggested that to ensure they had at least one French girl coming out at the ball perhaps the de la Rocques should be offered a table for ten and the younger girl a place among the debutantes. Underwriting the family would be necessary, everyone thought, as it was very doubtful that the de la Rocques would be able to afford it otherwise. She added, "You know this is a very good family, and they are quite well known in New York, but a professor's salary doesn't lend itself to international balls."

This seemed like a good move to Mr. and Mrs. Schlatz and everyone agreed that this was a great idea; this girl would symbolize both America and France – no one was very confident they were going to pick up any real French debs. The secretary said she would contact the family with this proposal and they could be listed as Patrons in the programme book.

It was in this way that Beatrice de la Rocque (Tourbonnière) came to be included – although perhaps in a homemade dress – in the affair of the I Love Paris Ball.

Chapter 2

I had no idea when I began this assignment and found myself in the Ritz lobby that day that I would be recording not just the origins of the I Love Paris Ball, but that of a new royal on the world stage, as well as the making of the most talked-about movie of the year, a big scoop for me – and all because Clarky Finch came into the Ritz that June afternoon.

A word about the Ritz: This was not the Ritz you see today; it was the Ritz before it was bought and $400 million-plus was spent renovating it, with new prices that excluded much of its old clientele.

At the time of this story, in the sixties, the Ritz was still just the best hotel in Paris, a place where you could meet your friends and see who had arrived in town; a place where ladies would come for tea, just as they would have done at that time at the Plaza in New York, and where they still can do at Claridges in London.

For me this assignment – an international story with an unusual angle – was a pleasant change, and I had decided to introduce my story with a picture of one of the debutantes. This would be the de la Rocque girl, who represented both America and France, and I was waiting in the lounge for her with my cameraman. As I ordered tea I looked around for familiar faces, or those that I should know – other than Clarky Finch. I recognized Clarky, of course, and made a note on my pad about his being in Paris; I could use it for my weekly *Where Are They Now?* column.

I did not know de la Rocques, although we had all agreed that the nineteen year-old, Beatrice, was to be the French representative until others could be found.

But when Beatrice de la Rocque came into the lounge she was something of a surprise. This was no ordinary girl – she was a classically beautiful one. Her looks were remarkable and she had inherited from some forgotten ancestor a figure that wafted, rather than walked; she was slender and quite tall; she was fair without artificiality, with chiseled, classical features and interesting dark brows.

She had large blue eyes that – either because she was short-sighted or because she was not particularly interested in her surroundings – seemed to look past everything, but she also looked pleasant.

She came through the lobby, past the rose-colored pink petit-point chairs, accompanied, or rather followed, by her mother and sister. One hand led a small Pekinese dog, who restrained her for a moment with the idea of chewing on the gilded tassels that formed the Ritz draperies. I could sense my cameraman's enthusiasm to be on such an assignment.

As she came toward us three waiters backed out of her way, and the wife of a Greek shipping tycoon suddenly felt she had allowed her hairdresser to overbleach her hair; the nineteen year-old American girl, who had just had her marriage annulled and was having early cocktails with her mother, straightened the skirt around legs which suddenly felt fat and short. At another table an English viscountess, mistress of a Labor peer, knew she would have made the mistake of nodding to the waiters, while this girl seemed not to notice them at all.

I was to learn that she was totally unaware of all this and was, indeed, very short sighted. Nor was the dog an affectation; she explained as we shook hands that she had had to bring her dog, Chong Sam, because he was really still only a puppy – there was no one to leave him with and he had to be watched or he chewed on things.

As we arranged for the picture, her sister and mother sat discreetly at a table nearby. It was a good picture and it would turn out that she was not only good looking but photogenic. We placed her chair against a tapestry holding Chong Sam. I thought he was cute – part lion, part chrysanthemum – and kept him in the picture. He seemed to know he had a role to play, which, in fact, he would.

The picture turned out worth making a full quarter page with my *Where Are They Now*? column – part of the prominence we had promised to the Schlatzes.

It was then that Clarky Finch and Alex Feldenstein came through the lobby with the vague idea that they might see someone they knew. It was a bit early to head straight for the bar.

The lobby of the Ritz was somewhat deceptive in those days. Half the people there were not guests of the hotel at all, but only there to be seen; some just used it to buy stamps from the concierge or even theatre tickets.

For instance, Clarky's family owned a large section of Manhattan and he received a monthly dividend check from a multi-million trust for more money than he could spend – if it wasn't for the fact that Clarky disliked spending any money at all. He was known to live in constant dread of spending his money and always took a room in a small hotel near Les Invalides that he was shy about naming. During his summer visits in Paris, however, he could be seen in the Ritz anxiously reading his bank statement prepared by the Morgan Guaranty across the Place Vendôme.

The management of the hotel had no objection to Clarky's generation making use of the hotel in this way, as one day they would grow up, marry, and take third floor suites with a corner window.

Also, they always drank Scotch, which has always been a major source of revenue for a hotel in France.

The previous year the management had even turned a blind eye to Clarky and a friend changing into black tie in the downstairs cloak room and leaving their things in a stall which they marked "Out of Order." Young people wore black-tie in those long ago days.

The management calculated that the presence of these young people off-set some of the clientele that the 20th century had forced on them.

We had finished the shoot and I was putting away our cameras when they saw us; both Clarky and Alex seemed attracted by the sight of cameras. But there was more – Clarky recognized Beatrice from New York. He didn't seem to be at all surprised to see her – to Clarky life was always a bit un-understandable, and as a result full of surprises that somehow didn't surprise.

Beatrice said to her sister, "Don't look now, but I think that's Clarky Finch. It is. He's coming over," then added, "What would he be doing at such an expensive hotel? He never spends a penny he doesn't have to."

"Hi there," Clarky said, and smiled.

In fact, seeing Beatrice made Clarky turn a brownish red and the smile was a defeated smile. Even now when he sees her photographs he feels like that.

Having his elbow jogged, he said, "This is Alex Feldenstein – Beatrice de la Rocque."

As I knew Clarky somewhat, I closed up my notebooks, saying, "de la Rocque Tourbonnière, you know, Clarkson," and moved over to the table from which Beatrice's mother and sister had been watching.

Alex Feldenstein said "Tourbonnière." His mind had gone to work in a way that would have been a real comfort to the woman from the Alliance for Arts and Culture in New York, who felt it was difficult to explain French society to Americans. Alex, like his father and uncles, owners of galleries in Paris and New York, were very aware of the various segments of any society.

The Feldenstein Gallery on the Faubourg St. Honoré was host, client and seller to the entire gamut of the international social world. At their exhibitions and sales one could see everyone from the super-rich of the Middle East buying up celebrated Italian Renaissance paintings – or their expertly disguised copies. One could see travellers from wherever there were collectors with money enough to buy something with a recognizable signature, and then just the artistically curious.

There was, however, another group even more important about whom they had to know: coming from England and the depths of the French countryside there were old families forced to dispose of heirlooms when faced with inheritance taxes in Britain and legal requirements to divide legacies in France. The Feldensteins were familiar with these old names with lost fortunes. They were a valuable source of things to sell.

Stroking back his almost frizzy reddish hair he said, "Toubonnière" again. The name de la Rocque Tourbonnière was recognizable to him, as someone who had passed the French *Bac*. He knew that it had more authenticity than Napoleonic titles, or mere Papal ones. There had been a Tourbonnière who had made a speech at the foot of the guillotine in 1793 that all French schoolboys had to learn by heart; a Tourbonnière had been rewarded with an estate on the Loire for having got rid of a lesser member of the Guise family during the religious wars in 16-something.

There was also a de la Rocque Églantin, a branch of the same family, who had given their name to a breed of green falcons in the late Middle Ages – a color which is known in decorator's jargon as Eglantine Green – a sort of avocado color. Alex looked thoughtful.

I heard Clarky say "What are you over for?"

She said, "The I Love Paris Ball."

"What's that?"

"It's a coming-out party"

"Oh."

Asked what he was doing in Paris, Clarky sat down. He had a vision of his day. It had started at 11:30 and included not knowing how much to tip the waiter at the café where he had breakfast; then having lunch at Fouquets, hoping he might see someone he knew and hadn't; it had cost him a fortune and left him at 2:30 with nothing to do; at 4 he had gone round to the Feldenstein gallery to see Alex, where he had picked him up and driven him to the Place Vendôme in his Mercedes.

This put him in mind of something he could say. He said, "I saw Nevsky yesterday, he said he was coming over here." And it was at this point that Ivan Nevsky came into the hotel.

A word is required to explain this young man whose name had occasionally appeared in my "*Where Are They Now*?" column, or if not his, certainly his mother's.

Ivan belonged to the New York and Long Island set through his mother, the three times married Eleanor Payne Glenn – heiress to Amalgamated Foods and rapidly approaching the alcoholic fringe.

His father, Prince Igor Nevsky had been her only husband to die. He had shot himself playing Russian roulette with a fellow Russian in a night club later torn down by developers. It was called the Waltzing

White Bear and was much patronized by Russians in those days. It was owned by Dmitri Tamorov, who claimed close kinship with the Romanovs.

By an accident of fate and genetics, Ivan had inherited an IQ far superior to anyone in his family or, to their discomfort, any of his professors – perhaps, some said, simply because he was Russian. This made him self-conscious about being an intellectual. He gave the impression that the ghosts of Dostoevsky and Chekhov, accompanied him much of the time.

That summer he had taken rooms on the Left Bank and would tell his fellow Americans that he was doing philosophy courses there, but it was more likely that he was just hanging around.

Ivan was amusing and arrogant. He had two attitudes – in scholarly moods he wore an old sweater and sat in cafés discussing Sartre, Rilke and Rimbaud late into the night. The girls he knew in these moods wore tight trousers, shaggy hair and white faces, and all had read the early works of Simone de Beauvoir, as everyone did in those days. Having met him they were emphatic about their belief in feminine freedom from bourgeois inhibitions. It amused Ivan, when he made them prove it, that without having read any de Beauvoir the girls he knew in New York reacted to him in the same way.

Throughout this society Ivan was thought to be a near genius, glamorously unpredictable; someone who read and sometimes studied. He was someone who drove like a professional, or at least very fast, and was irresistible to women, so the rumour went. This rumour made their conquest all the easier.

Of course there were many who rolled their eyes and said he was a jerk and a phoney, but even among those there was the suspicion that maybe he was actually somebody, and would admit he had a sense of humour.

He had, in fact, a reason for coming to the hotel that afternoon. His mother was arriving in a day or two and he had been told to see the receptionist about the room she liked and to remind them she would be having people for cocktails and to make sure the room she liked for that was available. She would want a waiter, hors d'oeuvres, cigarettes and flowers.

Every summer Eleanor Payne Glenn would arrive in Paris for a three-week stay at the Ritz with a mass of matching luggage. That summer it was the Black Watch tartan. She crossed by the French line and was met at the Gare St. Lazare by a limousine.

A great deal had to be forgiven Ivan and his affectations when considering his mother.

Interestingly, Mrs. Glenn did not have the appearance of a near alcoholic although it was, in fact, the case. Even now she does not. She is one of those women we used to see in High Society who in maturity adopted an old guard pose without abandoning, or regretting, the vices of their youth. They had grown a bit stout, with blue or blonde hair and were chauffeur-driven; they were sticklers for conformity, if not propriety. The blue hair rinse was one of those signs of the times that has totally disappeared, but was ubiquitous at the time.

These women entertained a succession of companions that ranged from unsuccessful actors, non-productive artists, courts of homosexuals, to old-fashioned gigolos. The more conservative of them continued to marry into their late 80s. They lived in mansions in those days when there were still servants; they voted Republican and felt they represented a dying order of American aristocrats. Their mouths had the slightly limp quality of the drinker or the toothless.

This social phenomenon was very American and not always understood abroad. The decadent British aristocracy would fling away appearances and remain racy into old age, often in company with horse trainers or kennel breeders. French sinners remained in a society of sinners, a classless circle that adhered to each other with a common philosophy of frankly admitted hedonism.

But at fifty-five Eleanor Payne Glenn claimed all her rights as a matron and often thought of herself as a widow, having had a husband that had died; that was Ivan's father. Often between marriages, and other arrangements, her mind would revert to Igor Nevsky; whenever that happened she used to put his picture in the drawing room and talk of him as "my late husband."

It was during these between-marriage moments that Mrs. Glenn, as she was actually known to her acquaintance, would take back her title of Princess Nevsky and complain of the alimony that two of her ex-husbands claimed. Each time she signed her name of the moment in the courthouse with a new husband, her friends would say,

"Isn't it wonderful? Did you hear about Eleanor? I'm so happy for her."

That summer – the summer of the I Love Paris Ball – Mrs. Glenn did not yet have blue hair; it was a pale metallic blonde, but she had already taken on a manner of grandeur that she had adopted after putting on weight, and which gave her a look of stability.

It is difficult to imagine her drunk until you have seen it. It consisted of sitting in a matronly sort of armchair, her feet on a footstool with a bottle of Old Grand Dad at her elbow, a bottle that steadily emptied. During this process she would discourse on the sloppiness of the dress and manners of the young – particularly her own son, and on the decline of the exclusivity of New York society. As she approached incoherence, she would name-drop her great-grandparents and the old man who had founded Amalgamated Foods. Before she passed out, she would mourn her governess, her old Long Island home, the racing stable and the days when there were only ten families in Palm Beach. Her companion of the moment would call the butler and together they would help her to her bedroom.

She also drank something in the morning, of course, and had white wine with lunch. Sometimes it was obvious that she had trouble with door handles and occasionally she cursed. She always made sense when she called her broker, however, or her banker, and she never confused names; her bills and businesses correspondence had been handled by attorneys for years.

For some time having people in for drinks had been her only form of entertaining – dinner being complicated and certainly too much trouble. And she liked to see her friends in Paris. It was in preparation for her coming that Ivan had come to the Ritz.

It is hard to say whether Ivan loved his mother or not; his feelings were ambivalent – veering from loyalty to embarrassment.

Although he had been put into boarding schools most of his life, there had been the summers when they had travelled about together from place to place; he had enjoyed that, and could remember a time when – still a child – he had felt like her champion.

He could remember his father's mother, too – old Princess Irina. The princess had a little dress shop in New York, and the afternoons he had spent with her as a child were timeless pleasant ones. He hadn't minded when she gave him a little icon and asked him to say his prayers.

It was six o'clock when Ivan came in. We saw him stand for a few moments considering his surroundings, looking sardonic in his old sweater, slim leather trousers and hair that hadn't been cut since he got to Paris. He obviously enjoyed feeling out of place.

Although he would inherit a large fortune one day with Amalgamated Foods or might even have been capable of earning one, in this Bohemian mood he pretended to say he thought luxury was corrupt. He had certainly been given every opportunity for judging as he had been with his mother to most of the world's playgrounds ever since he could remember.

Having spoken with the concierge for his mother he came over to Clarky.

"Who are your friends, Clarky?"

Clarky made the introductions, but Alex Feldenstein was still thinking as an art merchant, and continued his conversation with Beatrice:

"What kind of place is Tourbonnière? Will you be staying there later?," but her sister had answered,

"Well, we will go there to see our great aunt, I suppose. She is the one who lives there. It's in Normandy."

"Can we come, too?," asked Ivan, taking over the conversation. "Why don't we all go?"

"It's just a very old house." She was amused, "It's in terrible shape. No one has done anything to it for years, and it was damaged by Germans who occupied it during the war."

"How old?"

"Oh, late 17th century, I suppose, but part is older; it was originally fortified, I think. It has a crumbling tower in the back." She laughed, "Maybe that is why we are called Tourbonnière."

"We'll come and meet the great aunty," said Ivan. "It's just what we need, a medieval tower to lock Clarky up in."

Beatrice was not paying attention – she was ordering a pastry for Chong Sam. She thought they might as well have stayed in New York, at this rate. Chong Sam could not decide if he liked Clarky or not; he considered showing his feelings by making a puddle but decided against it. He curled up instead under a small table, considering Clarky's legs as he listened to the talk above him.

I made a note of these young people. I could use some of this in my column, and I nodded to my camera man to take a candid of the group.

Ivan said to Clarky, "Who's in town?"

Clarky remembered what he wanted to say:

"Alex says Tina Kraznik's in town."

To his annoyance, Ivan said, "Oh I know Tina – she was a top model; you see her around. Let's go and see her."

"She throwing a party?"

"No, she's just over at the George V."

"What about Sam?"

"In London. Movie premiere."

"What's the movie?"

"Spies, I guess."

"Any good?"

"Panned at New York previews."

"Whose she with?"

"Ask Alex."

Resorted to, Alex said, "She's here waiting for Sam. She says he's supposed to come and make plans for a movie in France." The Feldensteins had got to know the Krazniks over a painting sale.

"Do you know her, Nevsky?"

Of course, Ivan had at least met Tina Kraznik and he had seen her several times the year before in Torremolinos. She had been without

Sam at that time, too, but was rarely alone. In Paris she would be involved with movie people and any Jet Set personalities she ran into.

There was a certain competition going on between these boys over who knew Tina. Beatrice's sister, apparently called Francesca, had come over from where she sat with her mother, in what looked like a slightly protective way, and said,

"Who is that?"

"Sam Kraznik's wife."

"Who's that?"

"Movie producer/director."

Both Clarky Finch and Ivan Nevsky had the cash, the looks and the suitable genealogical confusion to make them part of the Jet Set that used to range from New York to Paris, to London and Mexico. Clarky's money alone, aside from his car, made him eligible for this stratum of society. It was a society which carried on its activities rather like the new British mods or surfers.

But their precocity and rashness, boys and girls alike, disturbed Clarky slightly; it was a form of cowardice or gentleness – or some decency of which he was equally ashamed – that made him half-hearted about it all and made him wish to know a less fast society.

In private he admitted to himself that he preferred a girl like Beatrice to chasing after a has-been model. Or frankly, the bright young things of the moment that flipped out their streaked hair behind speeding Ferraris which took them down to St. Tropez for the day.

Ivan, on the other hand, was part Russian, and his literary streak had led him to cultivate the Left Bank intellectuals when he was in France. He had a nebulous ambition of being known on his own intellectual merits one day – maybe as a writer. He assumed a recognition for excellence would come about as naturally and as effortlessly as his IQ had done. In this way he recognized his own potential without imagining he was supposed to do anything about it, like work.

In Europe he divided his time between attending Ionesco plays in his old sweater and suddenly driving to Geneva to see someone, when he affected an ascot and white silk suit made for him in Rome. Ivan Nevsky had made himself a remarkable reputation doing this.

In those days the younger set, like their parents, had a communication code that consisted in skillful name-dropping, as they were doing at this moment in the Ritz.

Now Ivan said, ‘OK, Alex, lets all go over and see Tina.”

Clarky demurred; she would be out or going out.

“Not this early, come one, come all, I need to drop off an invite to my mother’s drinks. We can get something to eat after.”

Alex had no objection. Tina and her husband were clients.

“OK,” he said “I’m game.”

I saw the boys round up the two girls, who looked amused; they waved at their mother. The grown ups around rolled their eyes.

****

Meanwhile, Tina Kraznik sat in room 222 of the Hotel George V wrapped in an enormous Turkish towel, and sipped champagne. She was looking at the six vases of tall stemmed roses that filled the room.

The tallest of these were from Sam and that was a bad sign. It meant that the *Eastward by Night* star was attractive and he was staying on in London to try to persuade her to do *Breath of Drums.*

Tina wondered whether she should quickly order some safari dresses while she was in Paris in case she went on location with Sam. *Breath of Drums* was to be filmed in Kenya and the National Park in part of South Africa. She would need some of those white canvas dresses with pockets and leather buttons, and a pith helmet. On the other hand, perhaps she would be divorced by that time. It all depended on whether they found a good location for the filming of *Les Cousines.*

For those who missed it, the film – later released in the United States as *By Kiss and By Kin* – which was written by a Frenchman, who has since entered Parliament as a Socialist – tells a touching but unsavoury story of incest and incipient lesbianism in a decaying French château. The book was praised by critics and loathed by anyone who owned a decaying château. Kraznik saw it as a chance to capitalize on the Tennessee Williams mood currently on the rise in Hollywood and funds that could not be taken out of France.

Tina had been married to Sam Kraznik for two and a half years. It was evident how unsuccessful her own career had been that she was known as Tina Kraznik rather than as Tina Vance, the name her modeling agent had chosen for her ten years earlier.

Nothing had ever quite clicked in Tina's life – she had nearly been the nation's top model; she had nearly made the movies. She had got with some difficulty and use of connections a bit part in *On the Rooftops*, but it hadn't led anywhere, and her marriage to Kraznik hadn't got her any further career-wise, either.

Marriage to Sam had been worthwhile in a way – she had travelled, of course, met people, swum at the Eden Roc and shopped in Paris, but she could tell that it was over. It would be difficult to reactivate her career now. She was known as Tina Kraznik, she was thirty-one and no one really makes it over thirty from what she had seen. She was beautiful enough; no one had ever doubted that; she just couldn't act.

Tina faced up to the fact that the money was going to have to come from someone. Kraznik could be counted on for several hundred thousand (in the sixties this was still a lot of money), but probably not more – he was already paying alimony to his two previous wives.

She didn't want to be kept. She'd tried that once and it was too binding. Next time it was marriage again or a deal where she could date, as she called it – unless she could think of some other way.

There were a couple of women that Tina felt had really known how to play their hands. All of them were well known, most of them had started as models as she had done. One, an English model, was now a Duchess; another a Serene Highness, whatever that was, and another she had read about was living in Switzerland, the second wife of a German Baron, who was in the news all the time. Those girls had really known how to bring it off.

Since she had been a teenager in South Carolina, named Betty Lou Cook, and had seen a movie called *The Loves of Princess Lana*, Tina had known what kind of life she really wanted. Princess Lana had worn a three-cornered hat and a riding habit; had had marvelous adventures in Italian gardens and savage forests, constantly surrounded by loyal retainers, accompanied by Italian greyhounds and courted by a masked swordsman. Somehow Tina had been looking for that ever since.

It was why, perhaps, she had envied those members of her profession who had married titles. She felt it was typical of her kind of luck that the only legitimate royal she had ever met was Maximilian of Hesse-Zeitfelt, and she had met him after she had married Sam. Of course if she hadn't been married to Sam she would not have been in Torremolinos when Maximilian came through. She made a play for him while Sam flew home for a gallstone operation, but she had been disappointed in that he was completely modern and, as far as her relationship with him went, it was just a few dates and he seemed just the same as any other man.

She thought her trouble with Sam had gotten worse around that time. Someone had been talking and there had been a small mention in one of the movie magazines that said something about 'Maximilian, younger brother of King Peter of Kravonia, had been among those seen at the side of beautiful ex-model Tina Kraznik in Torremolinos this month."

She felt she hadn't had time to make it come to anything. Not that she liked him that much. Nor could she have said exactly where Kravonia was. The Baron von Ogstseb was more attractive, but he was recently married and she hadn't got anywhere there. Maximilian, on the other hand, had stayed an extra few days and when he left had sent her a small present.

Tina didn't take this as being paid off; she took it as booty. As a matter of fact, she was disappointed that she hadn't heard from him. She thought they had some sort of deal to meet in Paris. It would have been pretty simple as he said he always stayed at the Hotel Prince de Galles, next door, and Sam was busy in London; Tina guessed he got delayed.

This evening the Schwarzes were taking her to dinner with Ari Zappas. That brought back her spirits. Ari Zappas was a Greek movie actor who had had a small part in *I Pericles*, filmed near Athens the year before. Tina knew that his attentions to her were a manoeuvre to forward his own career, but he was company and she didn't care.

Besides, she could put a call through to Buddy Holzer he'd fix things up. Buddy Holzer was a photographer. He had been on *Let's Talk* magazine for a time. Now he was doing location shots in Spain. She had known him since her early days in New York and they had broken into things together. He had always lined her up with people who could help her. There are several names for men who do that for women, but Buddy had an odd devotion to Tina that was more that just mutual advancement. He was a bit sorry for her, knowing that the marvelous cheekbones, the flawless sultry mouth, the huge cavernous eyes which had made her career in photographic modeling would not last, and she was a vulnerable kid.

She would put a call through to Buddy.

****

At the Ritz, Ivan pushed the group along. Stepping outside he lifted his chin at a passing taxi, which brought it to a halt. In those days taxis were usually old Citröens with the silver chevrons on the front, they were large with interior seats you could lift up for extra passengers. He crammed everyone in and threw the puppy on Clarky's lap saying, "Driver, follow that pigeon, and got in in front. Clarky sneezed.

This was not at all what Clarky had in mind; even Clarky could see that you don't call on models in their suites in the George V like this. To Clarky, Paris was meant to be a place that would satisfy a profound depth of curiosity about how other people – the really sophisticated people – live and carry on. He would not have put it quite like that. Perhaps he would have that in Paris people have really interesting lives; or he might have said that in Paris anything goes. He had heard, as everyone had, about what sort of parties are given there. He had read a book – he couldn't remember the title – about a club to which married people belonged that had a little membership key that they always wore around their necks and there were only red lights in their club, and no one asked anyone else's name and the things that went on in there were pretty far out.

Then there had been the diary of some fellow who was homosexual and heterosexual and just about every kind of sexual one can think of, who knew all the 'in' people on a first name basis, and more than that if you believed what was said. He wrote things too – songs or operas or something. And he had described gatherings, in a published diary, if you believed what he said. And he had been to places where just about every kind of game was played.

The trouble was that he just somehow never got invited to this kind of party, and sometimes he wondered if perhaps any of this actually existed.

He had been to shows in Pigalle, but the only people that weren't on stage seemed to be out-of-town businessmen or American servicemen, and the strip shows were just strip when you got right down to it. Clarky felt as if he had missed a turning somewhere.

What made the situation worse, was that he couldn't ask his friends what they knew as it would give away his own ignorance, and he was by far the richest of his friends and a few years older.

He was a little shamefaced about it all.

And now, here was this idiot Ivan Nevsky hauling him off to see an ex-model none of them knew worth a damn. His idea of calling on a film personality in their hotel rooms, for instance, was to appear at their door holding flowers, kiss them behind the ear while murmuring something smooth, and to settle down for a pretty sophisticated session of watching them get dressed to go out. In Paris, he knew perfectly well that this kind of thing would be done better than anywhere else – the furniture for one thing.

Now that makes a difference. To sit on a gilt chair with curly legs, surrounded by lace and marquetry furniture and draped hangings, goes a long way to making the whole thing more exciting. It in no way compared, for instance, to lounging on his mother's bed in the Park Avenue apartment while she told him that she wouldn't pay his parking fines again that winter, as she put on her arch support shoes. Nor did it compare to the occasional raids he had made into the girls' dormitory at school, or the times that his New York girlfriends had him over when their parents were out and you could hear them going in the children's room.

At this point Tina had told the operator to put through a call to Buddy Holzer. (In those days that was how you made long distance calls.) Buddy would help and Clarky was trying to get rid of his troublesome companions.

"We could just go somewhere for something to eat."

"Sorry, Finch, we're not that easy to get rid of."

"She probably won't be there."

"She'll be there; she'll be getting ready to go out."

"Oh my God," Clarky sneezed again. "I forgot my car."

"What car?"

"My Mercedes SL."

"No kidding. Do you have an SL? How does she handle?"

"Well, it's new." Clarky wasn't too sure about that. He usually drove rather carefully.

"What about oil? I'd take a Ferrari anytime. The one I smashed up last summer was a fantastic little car. It could do anything. I got her up to 180 before we went over."

"Who's was that?"

"Some guy in upstate New York. Don't remember who. God, was his mother mad: I'll never forget her face when she saw the car?"

Beatrice was bored by all this. She was squeezed in between Clarky and Ivan. It was almost impossible to keep her knee away from Clarky. They should not have agreed to going to see someone called Tina, whose husband was out of town, anyway. Francesca, on the other hand, was vaguely amused and didn't like her younger sister going around alone with entertaining wise guys in a city which they really didn't know.

The taxi stopped in the Avenue George V and Ivan said, "You'd better handle this, Finch. I haven't got a thing on me."

Ivan packed them into the elevator and Clarky found he was expected to continue to hold the dog. Chong Sam was not used to Paris elevators and became stiff and unyielding. Clarky sneezed again and the elevator rose painfully to the second floor. They knocked on number 222. There was no answer. They knocked again. Ivan said, "Tell them I knocked, said the stranger, knocked and nobody came."

Clarky suspected he was quoting something and felt uneasy.

"C'mon Nevsky let's get out of here."

"Come on out, Tina, We know you're in there," sang out Ivan.

"Come on Nevsky. She's out."

He noticed that the girls had got kind of silent.

"I hate to be a party-pooper, intervened Alex, who had said not much up until then, and felt like the only adult in the room, "We're in the wrong hotel."

In the lobby Ivan stopped them.

"My God, Finch, look at that. He's right. This is the Prince de Galles. Fine guide you turned out to be."

Ivan was saying to the desk clerk, "We will try to stay longer another time, my good fellow. We've an urgent commitment."

Tina was out of the Turkish towel by the time they knocked on her door. She was about to affix eyelashes. When she opened door she looked surprised and said, "Well, if it isn't the whole gang," and "Hi there," when introduced to the girls.

Her call to Spain had still not come through. She said, "Call for drinks while I get fixed," and disappeared in to do the eyelashes.

Ivan read the cards on all the roses. He showed some of them to Francesca, whom he thought looked clever and had some personality. Chong Sam went under the bed where he found some delicious tassels on a pair of silk slippers.

Tina called out, "you should see who I've got coming tonight."

"Who's that?" Ivan shouted while getting the puppy out from under the bed. Chong Sam had decided he didn't like this room. His mistress had been neglecting him and the perfume hurt his nose. He was looking about for a good place to show what he felt about it all.

"Ari," she shouted back. "Have you seen Ari Zappas?"

None of them had.

"He's Greek," yelled Tina. "He's a Greek Marlon Brando."

Francesca put the slippers far back in the closet. They weren't only chewed; where they were chewed they were gooey.

Tina came out. She sprayed her hair and did up her suspenders (in those days women had stockings held up with garter straps). She cancelled her call to Spain; she'd give it a try another time.

Tina had some time to spare before her date with Ari, so she sat down, lipstick in hand to make conversation.

"So what are you over for?" she asked the de la Rocque girls.

Ivan responded: "They are going to help me lock Clarky up in a tower they have."

Francesca, smiled. "My sister is coming out at a ball of some kind."

"No, no," said Ivan. "You promised we could all go and visit aunty and see the tower."

"You have a tower?" asked Tina. A tower was what Sam needed for the French movie. And keeping Sam in France to make the movie was what she wanted to do.

"He's being silly. My great aunt has a very old house in Normandy and it has an old tower. That's all."

Now it was Alex's turn to say something: "They are being modest. Their family has been around for centuries. So has the château. Is it registered as historic?"

"I don't think so; it's very out-of-the-way."

Tina: "What kind of tower? Can you go up in it?"

"Oh, yes, but it's very old and abandoned. It's quite hazardous; you know. It has a turning stair up to not much at the top. Just a big room. It's not at all glamorous."

Tina's attention was caught. What if it was something? She had heard Sam say often enough that they would have to find a tower to film the big scene on location.

The telephone rang, the Schwarzes were downstairs. The group went off to find a steak and chips in a sidewalk restaurant.

One would not have thought the evening would have been worth remembering.

****

When the de la Rocque girls left the hotel they found their way back to the apartment in the 8ème *arrondissement* found for them by their father's elderly aunt, Mme. de Lespinasse. Of course this lady was not really their aunt at all, although she was a sister of the aunt by marriage who lived at Tourbonnière. She was a connection through marriage with a second cousin of their father's, a gentleman long since passed away. But among traditional French families this could be considered a close connection.

Madame de Lespinasse, who dressed always in black, was a member of that French society that the woman from the Alliance for Arts and Culture had in mind when she shook her head at the meeting with Bilco Oil. She was someone about whom visitors to Paris would not normally see or know anything about.

A child during the First World War, born to an old family in "straitened circumstances," as we used to say, she had married François de Lespinasse during the twenties; she had had no children before he passed away while still quite a young man.

On a minute income she had inhabited her apartment near the Rond Point ever since. She was there all through the Second War and the throes of the German occupation – a period during which some of her relatives had simply kept their heads down – some had joined the Free French in North Africa – and some had quite openly worked with the Vichy government.

She never referred to those times at all and as normal life returned – after the Americans had left, as she would say – she had gone on with an even smaller income doing what she thought her duty. She also did what she thought were kindnesses and which were often thought meddling. She was devout, limited and had beautiful manners.

It was this kindly lady who had pointed out to the de la Rocque family the availability of an apartment in her building, an apartment belonging to friends who had gone into the country.

Francesca and Beatrice left the George V, making their way toward this temporary home, shaking their heads over the coincidence of seeing Clarky and being dragged off to see Tina Kraznik. They agreed they might as well have stayed in New York. They reached the building and as quietly as possible made their way to the elevator.

Now in France elevators have personalities all of their own. Otis has not imposed a frozen uniformity on them. French elevators speak to one of *les grandes cocottes* who have ridden in them, of Prince Danilo and Maxims, and more recently of Nazi officers.

These elevators reflect the personalities of the concierge; they sigh that things are no longer as they were. Some creak a little like the old family retainer who has grown old in the service of the family, or the Marquis who knows he is the last of his line. Some jerk importantly telling Monsieur that it will take Monsieur to the *troisième* since Monsieur insists, but Monsieur will probably not find Madame at home.

Some delicately wrought iron elevators, designed like gilded cages, oil their way discreetly, knowing better than to ask you why you come at that particular hour and much too knowing to tell you who it is that they just took away.

These elevators do not have telephones or squeeze muzak at you – they do not open automatically, wait one impatient moment and disappear; on the contrary, they expect you to carefully open two narrow glass doors, reach out to the wrought iron and mildly gilded handle and let yourself out through the shaky gate. They do not rush you at express speed to the top floor when you want to only get to the 3rd. Nor do Parisian elevators say: "Inspected in 1955 by supervisor John Black," whoever he was – is he Swiss that one can trust his supervision? No, French elevators were not inspected. If Monsieur is not satisfied with it, if Monsieur does not care for the elevator, Monsieur can take the stairs.

The girls tiptoed their way not to disturb Mme. de Lespinasse, or their mother, certainly back by now, but also not to have to explain where they had been. How could anyone explain Tina Kraznik to Tante de Lespinasse?

La Tante had made herself busy wondering how she could get the girls introduced to suitable young men, looking through her handwritten genealogies to find suitable families; she had no opinion about *le bal Americain.* Downstairs on the second floor there was the Buisson Fleuri family, but all those boys were too young to be of use.

Chapter 3

At my magazine we had been told that the Duc de Ruissy had, indeed, asked his mother, the Dowager Duchess, to stand in as Chairman of the I Love Paris Ball, just as Mr. Schlatz had said.

I learned as a follow-through that the Duchess had agreed to meet with Charlotte Schlemmer, as mentioned at our New York meeting, and that she had invited the Duchess to lunch at Joseph's, where they ordered omelette, salad and vin rosé.

In fact, nothing at all would have happened and there would have been no I Love Paris Ball without the Schlemmers. She was thrilled with this project. It would suit her social ideas down to the ground.

Carl Schlemmer was vice president and European representative of Bilco Oil, and on the day his wife was to meet with the Duchess he left Paris for a meeting of oil distributors in Nantes. As he shrugged himself into his overcoat at the door of his apartment, he told his wife that he just didn't seem to be able to explain to the home office that you can't rush Europeans... and they resent it if you try. Actually, the home office thought he had come to see things a bit too much from the European point of view.

At least since his time in Paris he had certainly become totally converted to a European way of life. He took two hours off for lunch every day, and since his last trip home had definitely decided on retirement in some part of France – if he could find just the right little estate. His recent trip to New York had shocked him. "New Yorkers have no idea how to live," he told Charlotte.

This was Charlotte Schlemmer's fifth consecutive year in Paris. Not her fifth year in the high ceilinged Avenue Victor Hugo apartment they now occupied, however. The Schlemmers had had a smaller one near the Parc Monceau when they had first taken over the Paris office, but she had soon realized that she would need more space if she was going to entertain, and an imposing address if she wanted to meet society.

Her husband's position as vice president of Bilco Oil was in many ways as positive and important a position as any diplomatic post in the European theatre, a fact fully recognized by the Embassy. Socially, she meant to make the position as accepted in Paris as that of the wife of the president of the Morgan Guaranty in the Place Vendôme, which she felt rivaled an Embassy in social value.

What with the French changing their mind continuously about American business and American dollars, her husband was an important behind-the-scenes man at the Quai d'Orsay, where a lot of important talks went on, as well as with the Common Market top men (In the sixties there was the Common Market long before the EU). In a way it was a marvellous position – so powerful, and with no ties to the State Department. You could tell by the condescending way that Mrs. Schlemmer talked and walked that she understood how important her husband's position was.

She had a V-shaped face and chic short grey hair, she wore rings with very large stones which flopped about while she arranged her cards at bridge or poured coffee. She and Carl had married late – she had been an advertising executive with the company and worked with teenage fashions before that. She had that alert, crisp intelligence that they like in France, but which branded her as a career woman, rather than society, in the United States.

It hadn't taken anyone as intelligent as Charlotte Schlemmer long to realize that she could create a position in Paris for herself that she could never have done in New York and only with great difficulty in Washington. She soon found out that she could make her position more than just one of the American Embassy crowd. She worked at her French and developed the ambition to form a salon – only it wasn't really a salon she had in mind: it was a series of small cocktail parties, with regulars who would make important international business decisions in her drawing room.

She had started by giving bridge parties for the Americans and the few French women that she knew in Paris. For the first two years she had served American salads, cake and coffee, but she had dropped that. Now that she had begun to get the hang of French society, she invited a slightly different crowd and hired a perfect Spanish maid who was a *cordon bleu*, who combined perfect French luncheons with things like *truite bleu,* as French people admire what they are already familiar with and, also, she came to prefer it that way herself.

French sophistication is not learnt – it is a form of contagion: one is either immune or vulnerable to it. If one is vulnerable to it one can become contaminated in a few months, or even from books. French sophistication is particularly appealing to clever people, which the Schlemmers both were. English sophistication is not in any way dependent on intelligence; it is therefore more universal and easier to imitate.

Charlotte Schlemmer had met Henriette de Ruissy as a matter of course through Bilco Oil, their husbands being in touch often. She had known how to make a friend of Henriette by an astute outlay of hospitality that the duchess enjoyed and yet which made no claim on her. Mrs. Schlemmer always invited Henriette to do things that are natural to a French leader of fashion and yet which they cannot always afford – seats to gala performances at the Opéra in honour of something ambassadorial, tickets to first showings of collections – and through the duchess she had learned to understand the Paris she wanted to know.

She had furnished her drawing room with Louis XVI chairs and a sky blue and grey carpet worth $10,000, which was a great deal of money at that time. She always got cut flowers from the market, and gradually she began to merge with France. She entertained cleverly, always having guests who had something to get from one of the other guests. She had begun to know artists, diplomats and business heads.

With her husband she had the ambition to buy a small country place in France one day; somewhere in the hunting country – probably Normandy. The idea of returning to New York was out. Her ambition included being a houseguest at Ruissy and to become something like a French landowner herself. There was nothing hypocritical about Charlotte; she just preferred France.

Nor was she a snob; she just had a clear knowledge of who was at the top and preferred them. Already after only a few years in Paris she had the perfect way of mentioning important names, as if only a nobody would think anything of it. Of course anyone who has survived the advertising and fashion business in New York can handle anyone, even the French.

She had come to know all the antique shops of the 13th *arrondissment* and was making some astute buys, with an eye to furnishing the place in the country one day.

She saw misty pictures in *Connaissance* magazine – blue and green and symphonies of yellow and green, showing off the charm of the place that she and Carl would one day own. She wanted it choice, small and very very French, with lattice woodwork somewhere, wrought iron gates and grey slate. She would have a paved terrace with bronze statues of the Seasons and yellow umbrellas for al fresco lunches.

She would have people like the Ruissys of course, and novelists, a minister or two. They would drive out for the day, perhaps, for a hunt meet, so the place would have to be not too far from Paris. Her parties would be European in that they would be a mixture of people – deceptive mixtures, who were uniform in their success. Charlotte Schlemmer had also learned the chic of having a priest included in small gatherings, and she often talked very interestingly about the Church; in fact, she was really interested in it, or thought she was. Her interest did not take her as far as attending religious services, but she had read the latest philosopher on the subject.

There was nothing insincere about Charlotte – she just knew what she liked and had a good idea of how to get it.

All of which is to say, she was delighted with the idea of the ball. She had not yet met the dowager duchess of Ruissy, who was to be the honorary chairman, and felt this would certainly consolidate her social position as a friend of the Ruissys.

Charlotte intended to make a huge success of it, especially as the French-American relationship was going though a difficult moment politically. Carl said they could make the affair a benefit for the Historic Monuments, of which the duke was president. It seemed a perfect idea from a public relations point of view; for an American company nothing could be better – certainly it would raise funds for the Historic Monuments and with the duchess as chairman its social acceptance was guaranteed.

The American girls would be flown to France through a special arrangement with the French airlines; that would be easy.

When they met, the two women went over what needed to be done to bring off the Schlatz ball. Charlotte's notes were all expertly typed up on an executive typewrite by her husband's secretary at the Bilco Oil office.

The charity ball, or more loosely the fundraiser, is one of those institutions that has something for everyone – at that time it was typically American; less common in Europe. Its advantages were many: the organizers of the affair gain a reputation for being active for others and they gain any amount of publicity; if they don't have the time or skill to do the work, they have a committee to do it for them. Now a committee member is called on to bear much less responsibility, but contribute a reasonable amount of money. Often, however, they are only asked to hand over their address books to the invitation committee.

In the United States those who take a table can deduct it from their income tax as a charitable contribution; and there is the advantage of entertaining guests with music, refreshments and decorations that they could not have afforded on their own. Further, depending on the size of their donation their name will be listed as a patron.

For those who can afford to take a party there is a special mention in the programme as a "Special Patron," or as a member of a miscellaneous committee.

For the artists who donate their time and talent to the charity there is, of course, only a small fee, euphemistically called an 'honorarium,' but if they are out of work, or "resting," they are glad of an engagement that might help them re-activate their career or make new contacts. Charlotte Schlemmer was aware of all this.

If, as in the case of the I Love Paris Ball, the event is to present debutantes, the girls receive much more publicity when presented at a charity function, the press being more prone to give publicity to a charity.

In those days, these parties involved leading names, and the organizers would find someone to whom the girls could be presented. Hopefully, this would be someone of sufficient celebrity in the opinion of the grandmothers, who helped foot the bill, to think it was worth getting their tiaras out of the bank, cleaned and insured for the day.

Mrs. Schlemmer's brain worked quickly. She had an idea for where the ball should take place. She thought immediately of the fabulously wealthy Fermin Ben Fazy, thought to be an Egyptian, who had bought an historic Hôtel Particulier in the old section of Paris known as Le Marais; it was in extremely bad repair and he was restoring it.

The Historic Monuments might be involved and it would be a wonderful place for the ball. It was no good wondering where his money came from and one didn't need to listen to those who said he was an arms dealer.

This idea seemed to bring a number of elements together, but how to attract young French people was another matter.

The Duchess and she made notes – she said perhaps her husband could organize for the cadets of both the elite Polytechnique and St. Cyr academies to form an honour guard for the party. This would be attractive and supply a number of young men – at least enough to dance with the eight or so girls taking part.

Mrs. Schlemmer knew the perfect caterer. She thought she could get the head chef of the Tour d'Ivoire to provide the dinner.

The ball began to take shape in her mind – music must be arranged and flowers.

****

The evening following the meeting the ducal family sat in the smaller salon of their Avenue Matignon apartment.

It is often said that the French do not allow strangers into their homes. That is because the French fit life into categories: they keep meeting places for friends, offices for business and the home for family.

They haven't evolved the American system of blending these things together at a club.

During this evening in the Ruissy apartment, for example, the older duchess put on comfortable shoes and played Patience with herself – she says it makes her sleep more easily. The duke usually sits at his desk and goes through the correspondence he couldn't answer during the day. On this particular evening he read the latest ultimatum from the tax adjuster. His wife, Henriette, normally makes sure that the young had done their homework; or if they had already gone into the country to her mother, which was, in fact, the case at this time, she does needlework.

The duke's younger brother, Gérard, sips brandy and reads the popular press. Their eldest son, Olivier, was home that evening, but would normally be out with friends.

The room in which they spend these evenings is a green color and is brooded over by the full-length portrait of the 17th century periwigged duc de Ruissy of that time. He has a broken nose, a gleaming cuirasse and a vague velvet arrangement. He dominates the room, the same way he dominated any room he entered in 1690; Sieur de Montplaisant, Baron de Toussaint, Comte de Beauvalet, Keeper of the King's Conscience, Grand Marshal of the French Armies and duc de Ruissy. In the lower left of the portrait is the family coat-of-arms; the simple chevrons of the oldest families, surmounted by a star and shell of the Crusaders. It is surrounded by one of the few ancient mottos in French heraldry, "*Quand je le veult*" (in old French: "When I want it").

In his time no one was ashamed of the distilled pride which was attached to power. They glorified it in portraits, like this one, with every prop and angle the artist could arrange. This portrait of the duc hangs in the Avenue Matignon apartment because there are two others at the castle and a bust in one of the museums – wearing a marble hat, plume and lace collar.

Opposite hangs his nephew, the Cardinal de Ruissy, with the same nose – though unbroken – and a shrewd eye. I do not know that he was famous for his sanctity, but wit, humour and learning served him well. Under his portrait is written: Joseph André, François, Cardinal de Ruissy, Grand Chaplain of France, Order of the Holy Spirit, 1661–1740.

No doubt a good man to know. Not long ago, Gérard de Ruissy found a slender leather-bound book dating from the period, written by this same man, on the practice of black magic and methods for its investigation.

On the floor of the smaller salon was an Aubusson carpet and the feet of some furniture that belonged to the Duchesse de Berry before her husband was assassinated in 1816.

On this evening, the young duchess threaded her needle with moss green wool and settled down for a comfortable evening of chat. It really didn't matter to Henriette de Ruissy that no one would answer what she said, or would listen much.

"*Alors, ma mère*," she said, "What did she have to tell, the Mrs. Schlemmer?" Her mother-in-law dealt herself an ace.

"We made arrangements, of course," she said, "And she talked about the Tourbonnière sisters, who are to represent France."

"*Comment?* which Tourbonnière? There are no Tourbonnière girls in Paris."

"But the girls of Xavier de la Rocque Tourbonnière, *ma fille*."

"Of America? Since when are they here? It is extraordinary that I hadn't heard."

The young duchess was not that pretty. However, she had certain attractiveness. She had rather a flat face like a clever monkey and bright, darting brown eyes. Nothing happens in her world of *tout Paris* that she doesn't instantly hear about, and about which she doesn't instantly have an opinion.

The older duchess said, "One can assume that Xavier wishes his daughters to know France. Perhaps marry here, after all."

"One asks oneself why," said the duke. He was half way down the assessment of his assets by the tax authorities.

The older duchess reshuffled, and told them that the family had taken an apartment in the rue de la Boétie through the kindness of Mme. de Lespinasse.

"*Pas possible*!" Henriette bit off her wool. "But he has become very rich, then, Xavier de la Rocque. He has made a fortune in America."

Her brother-in-law Gérard looked up from his newspaper to say all Americans were rich. They did not have to support the *sacré gouvernement* imposed in France. He said he foresaw the eventual ruin of his country. As he had said the same thing about the last twelve governments, no one paid any attention.

"It must cost something to bring his family to Paris for the season! *Un appartement! Le voyage!* You hear, *Chérie*?"

It had always grated on the Ruissys, how much Henriette talked about money.

Her husband nodded without looking up.

Gérard went on, "Xavier de la Rocque has done very well then *en Amérique...* All Americans were rich. That was why people went to America. He couldn't think of any other reason.

"According to Mme. de Lespinasse, who I saw the other day at St. Augustin," the older duchesse dealt again, "she wishes to arrange for the girls to meet suitable young men. *Des entrevues* for her nieces. To marry them here."

"But it is extraordinary! Do you hear, *chérie*?" Hervé de Ruissy's lips moved as he added a column of figures, but he nodded again.

Gérard said that he couldn't understand anyone wishing to return to France. The country was rotten with taxes. They were sure to have a Communist government before long.

"Are they well physically?" asked the young duchess. "They must have formidable dowries. It no longer exists in France. Really I find it extraordinary, don't you, *chérie,* that Xavier de la Rocque wishes to marry his daughters in France? Think what it must have cost. Are you listening, *Chérie*?"

"*Oui Henriette.*"

"How are they physically, *ma mere?*" French people are rather direct in referring to looks in this way. "It could be an interesting match for someone. *N'est pas, Chérie?*"

"According to Mme. de Lespinasse, the younger one is a *belle.*"

"*Pas possible*! But it is *formidable.* He wishes to marry them here in France! And they say that everything is easy in America! They say that in America everything is made easy!"

Gérard said that in present-day Paris, the only receptions worth going to from the point of view of food and wine were given by Americans.

His mother put down a nine of spades with a philosophical look. She had never been able to cure her younger son of being an epicure. Personally, she thought it vulgar.

"It is a shame that Olivier is not yet settled in a position," said the young duchess – "one could have considered one of them as a possibility."

"*Tu te rencontres,*" she went on, "that those girls are the great-nieces of the Marquis de Cochefôret through their grandmother... It would have been wonderful for Olivier, *Chérie*, and a fortune in America!"

"But the marquis has been dead for years," the duke was still counting. "I remember when Papa told me that he had died at the races."

"What difference does it make if the old marquis is dead? It changes nothing that he died at the races. They are still the nieces of the Marquis de Cochfôret. What will they have as dot? *Ma mère*?" She put on her glasses and threaded her needle with a dark red.

"I have no idea. The matter did not arise."

"*Chérie,*" Henriette glanced again at her husband over her glasses, "Perhaps M. de la Rocque wishes to move back to France. Perhaps he would like to buy Bellefontaine."

Bellefontaine was a small property in the Loire et Cher that the Ruissys felt they would have to sell.

"Me, I find it extraordinary that they wish to return to France. They say everything is so easy in America. They say everything has been done to render life easy. Everything is modern over there."

Gérard said that if he was returning to France, he would be more interested in restoring Tourbonnière than buying an expensive property in the Loire et Cher.

"That is an idea," Henriette looked up again.

The duke looked up and said to his mother, "*Ma Mère*, we will have to sell Bellefontaine. We are never going to find the sums they ask for. I see no other way."

Gérard said it was slavery; that they all became slaves of the government. It was the ruin of the country.

The older duchess said, "We will soon see what the girls are like when they are presented at the ball."

During this time the duke's son, Olivier, was reading in a corner of the room. Asked what he thought of meeting the girls from America he said he had not been listening. When called to attention he said, "But I have met plenty of American girls, you know."

Olivier had done the engineering courses at the elite Pont et Chaussée, the French technical college, and on graduating had been advised by his father to get a graduate degree from MIT; he was home on vacation from his first year in Boston.

His grandmother said, "*Voyons*! I am going to ask you to be my cavalier at this event, Olivier – at this ball for the Historic Monuments that these Americans are sponsoring. I count on you to give me your arm."

Olivier loved his grandmother, and said "*Avec plaisir, Bonne Maman,*" which explains how it came about that Olivier de Ruissy was seen at the I Love Paris Ball in the Hôtel de Plessis only a few weeks later.

This conversation also explains how it came about that the younger duchess made it her business to meet and work on the I Love Paris Ball with Charlotte Schlemmer – relieving her mother-law of any involvement with it other than appearing as its Senior Patron.

Chapter 4

During the time that the I Love Paris ball was thus in preparation, Helen, the Dowager Queen of Kravonia – sitting in the patio of her small villa in Cascais, clenched her fist with annoyance. Her clipping service had just sent her a small article mentioning her son's name in a Hollywood gossip magazine as being seen with a well known ex-model. What was she to do? Would he never understand and make himself useful?

Cascais, near Lisbon, had become a colony of ex-royals during the post-war years. As a resort it was quiet and elegant, not too expensive; there former kings, queens and princes sat around card tables playing canasta (a lot of canasta was played in those days) – a happy substitute for the many wars their respective ancestors had fought for generations.

She got out her pen to write.

A few days later, Maximilian Hohen-Zeitfest, younger brother of King Peter of Kravonia, stood in his hotel bedroom and swore. He was bored, angry and disgusted. He held two letters in his hand.

First among the letters he had found waiting for him in the hotel reception was one from his mother, the Dowager Queen, usually referred to as the Grand Duchess, Helen. Her letter came from Cascais, of course, where she was staying with her sister, Princess Alice Victoria.

Maximilian had spent the last ten years disliking his mother's letters – they were hardly ever complimentary and always told him the truth. The one he held now not only told him the truth, it was attached to a small clipping from an American movie magazine. The clipping was innocuous enough: it said that he had been seen in the company of the glamorous ex-model, Tina Kraznik, in Torremolinos the month before.

His mother's letter, however, was extremely frank; she said that the clipping service had sent her the enclosed and she was extremely troubled. She said that she realized that he had never understood the seriousness of his position, but could nothing convince him of the seriousness of his brother's?

She went on: she could understand his wish to have his own life, but could he not see that every piece of second-rate publicity he picked up reflected on his brother, who, he knew perfectly well, was doing an extremely difficult job as well and conscientiously as it could be done. She was shocked that she had to remind him of the precarious nature of constitutional monarchies, particularly at a time when the constitution was under review by a leftist government.

She didn't want to go into all that again, but an association ("association" was what people like Queen Helen called what Tina termed "dating") with married Hollywood personalities that got into the papers could easily mushroom. Did he think the tag "Playboy Prince" would help his brother? When he had been younger and simply wanted to race cars or fly aeroplanes, she had said nothing, because that could hurt only himself, and she was fully aware of the frustrations involved in being a second son, but now that he was in his thirties she was seriously vexed to think he still needed his mother to tell him where his responsibilities lay.

The letter went on like that.

Maximilian swore again, and being brought up as royalty he could swear in six languages, not the least useful being the language of the British Royal Navy in which he had served a stint, and where so many princelings had become men.

For years he had said he felt he was forced to live a life in which he was not allowed to play a real part; he could have no effective role in politics lest he compromise his brother, and he did not like co-operating with the damn fools who actually ran his country.

He almost envied his Austrian cousins who no longer occupied a throne and could know anyone they wanted to and who could have political views. He had watched his father and then his brother go through humiliating experiences with recalcitrant prime ministers while wearing their star and ribbon; standing beside low-lifes, who called themselves prime ministers, standing to attention for anthems that had spelt the death of close relations.

For thirty years he had hated his position, having only enjoyed the time in his uncle's navy, where he had been treated on his merits for a few wonderful years, and where he had been able to excel in mathematics and working as an officer without regard to his princely rank.

During those years Europe's gossip magazines had referred to him as Europe's "Prince Charming," but then he had been lectured by everyone around him for not marrying properly. Since then he had been called Europe's "Bachelor Prince" and had turned a deaf ear to what anyone said. Now that a Socialist government was in charge of the cabinet in Kravonia he was sometimes referred to by their own newspapers as "Our Playboy Prince." It was this that worried his mother more than anything. Only tact, usually her own, had saved the crown on more than one occasion. Furthermore, at this very moment they were vulnerable to a resurgence of an anti-monarchist campaign. Yet, as she repeated, only the monarchy could weld together the deep ethnic and religious differences in their country.

And Maximilian swore now, not only because he knew that his mother was right, but because in his other hand he held a note from Tina Kraznik whom he had forgotten all about.

But he also swore because it had come upon him recently that all the ways he spent his days bored him, and more than anything he wanted a change. He wanted something real, and worse, he had noticed lately that his hair was beginning to recede.

That afternoon Prince Maximilian went down to the hotel barber, wondering if there was something to be done about the hairline.

His bad temper and the feeling that something in his life had to change deepened. His life was becoming pointless and bitter. The fact that there was no door in Europe or America that was not open to him, that he belonged to one of the last surviving royal houses, that he had been courted by his royal kin as a possible groom for twenty female royal youngsters – and had managed to avoid them all, that he knew himself to be a handsome man of ability, as yet only in his mid-thirties, did not comfort him. Knowing those things never does. Besides, he had forgotten to take his antihistamine and had promised to go to represent the commercial interests of Kravonia at the opening of a major automobile show.

At least he knew and liked cars and it would please his mother.

****

That evening Tina Kraznik did not go out. She put a call through to Sam at the Savoy in London, but could not reach him. She was one of those women who sit around in their underthings when alone at home. Perhaps this was because she didn't have pretty frilly ones when she was growing up as Betty Lou Cook in North Carolina, or perhaps it was because of a theory she had read that you take better care of your shape if one is usually bare.

She was wearing French underthings now, ruffled pants and a bra with the ruffles on the inside. She was beginning to feel very lost.

Later in the morning she put a call through to Ivan Nevsky, whose telephone number was on the card he had given her concerning his mother's cocktail party.

Like a hundred other pseudo summer students he lay in his bed in his room near the Boul' Mich and re-read a page in his favorite book. He was re-reading James Joyce.

Madame Bonnard yelled up the stairs that he was wanted on the telephone and he gradually appeared on the top landing looking young and tousled, wrapped in his bedspread. He made a grimace at the telephone – it was of antique design.

Telephones in France were not designed for lengthy conversations in those days. There is even a theory that they were purposely designed by the Postal Service to discourage their use. The kind that Ivan picked up now had a foot of brass dowel between the mouth piece and the earpiece. Trying to use this kind of telephone used to make one hit one's lip alternately with banging the side of one's head.

There was an extra earphone that was meant to allow one to listen with both ears, but if one did this one had no hands left for holding the directory open, and when the operator asked what number she has disconnected you from, one had to look it up again with one's elbows. And anyway, in practice the extra earphone was used by the concierge to find out what you were talking about.

Ivan picked up the receiver with a weary look of experience and said, '*Allo* ?,' as one does in France. It was Tina.

Tina's voice was full of static, and as her mouth was full of breakfast, he found it difficult to hear.

Young men rarely want to be telephoned by women in the morning. He was no exception. He looked beseechingly at the ceiling. Why couldn't women learn that they would be called when they were wanted?

Tina explained that she had been unable to reach him the night before and that she was anxious to meet up with those two girls he had brought round to the hotel with Clarky Finch.

"Sam might want to take a look at their place."

He said he thought all she had to do was come to his mother's cocktail at the Ritz. He had asked them to come; they had said they would.

"*Ne quittez pas, ne quittez pas*" (Hang on, hang on), said the operator, and they were cut off.

She planned to go. She might have something to tell Sam.

But now she couldn't reach Sam and the Schwartzes with whom she had had dinner were gone and Ari Zappas had gone to a house party in Rome. She had thought of going with him, but that would be really asking for trouble at this point.

Buddy was right when he said if she thought that things were going bad with Sam that she should only be seen with people who would help her case. If it came to that, Ari was still not more than part gigolo.

She was worried and spent her time listening for the telephone, with the result she noticed the two lines from her nostrils to the corner of her mouth had reappeared. She smoothed on medicated mask advertised for re-toning facial muscles, and lay down on the bed. She decided that Buddy was right as usual. She should give Sam no more cause than he already had (Hell! – he might have been having her watched for all she knew), but at the same time Buddy had said it would be good to seen with Max.

This would be an ace up her sleeve. The divorce court would be a lot more generous toward a wife who had dated royalty while her husband was signing up stars in another city. Buddy was right about that, too. Tina had seen studio shots of the young star of *Eastward by Night,* who Sam now wanted for *Breath of Drums.*

She had the kind of beauty that Tina despised. She looked healthy and had a clear forthright look that Tina assumed was achieved by the way the makeup people penciled on the eyebrows. It was not a look she herself had been able to use.

Tina could not come up with a reason to explain Max not having called. She knew he was in Paris – for one thing he had told her in Torremolinos that he would be in Paris in June, and for another she had seen in a paper a small mention that he was due to be present at one of the big car showrooms that was presenting a new line of small cars assembled in his country. Further, she remembered he had said that he did not like staying at the embassy with his ambassador – who had voted against his father in '47 – and that he always stayed at the Hotel Prince de Galles.

She had phoned the place and they said they had him registered, but that he was not in; she wondered if he had got her note. And she thought of calling again to ask if he had picked up his mail. She wondered why he hadn't called. Oddly enough the only explanation that did not occur to her was that he hadn't called was because he didn't want to.

She began to pedicure her feet. Halfway through her left foot she decided to put another call through to Buddy. She forgot that Sam might want to know why there were so many calls put through to Spain. (In those days hotels put through calls which were registered for payment.)

It took a while to locate Buddy, by which time she had ordered herself champagne cocktails from downstairs and was in a half tearful state. No one had asked her out anywhere that night. People always thought that people like her were part of a gay crowd. No one knew how lonely she was. Now that she had had a few drinks her feelings overcame her usual concern about not to make her celebrated cavernous violet eyes swell up. Crying always produced two horizontal lines under them next day.

Buddy was her only friend. And she told him this rather blurredly when she reached him in the Spanish restaurant where he had gone with several other photographers and technicians. He was the only one that really cared what happened to her. Not Sam. Not her mother. Not any of the SOBs she had ever been with. Sam didn't love her. Nobody had ever cared about her but Buddy. They just wanted her body. No one but Buddy and whoever it was that had invented champagne.

She went on: no one realized that she was just a little girl – and her mother had never loved her, but she couldn't help who she was attached to, could she? That was physical. She could remember her mother bringing home all kinds of guys and giving her a licking when she peeked. Tina's accent became noticeably more Southern after her fourth glass.

Buddy spoke slowly and clearly. He wanted to know if there were any new developments. It made him mad when women started hitting the sauce!

Tina said there wasn't anything new excepting that she had called that little Nevsky guy and that he was fixing up for her to meet the two little virgins with the castle.

Buddy thought that sounded pretty good.

"Does Sam know about this, Honey?"

"I can't get him. I've left messages. He's probably living it up with some little… "

"OK, okay. Did you write to the Royalty?"

"Sure, Like you said."

"What happened?"

"Nothing happened. Like I told you."

"Did he get it?"

"I guess he must've."

"What did you tell him?"

"I told him I was at the George V and Sam was in London. So I had got kind of lonely and why didn't he come on over for a drink?"

"Who've you been seen around with?"

"I ain't been been seen around with nobody. Didn't I tell you already? Just Ari Zappas for a coupl'a dates."

Tina started to sob and Buddy gave her time before he told her he would be in Paris on his way through in a couple of days. Meanwhile, she was to try to see Max. He told her to have something to tell Sam about the *By Kiss* location and not to get discouraged.

Tina's champagne cocktails saw her through to an unconscious state that night. It was not a difficult thing for them to do, as she hardly ever ate anything to speak of. During her modeling days she had suffered from a dropped kidney due to drastic dieting and she had never had a proper digestive system since.

Buddy Holzer went back to his dinner of fried rice and shrimp, perturbed. He and Tina had both broken into the toughest business in the world and had always helped each out of tough situations. He had thought she had really gotten herself fixed up with Sam Kraznik. She shouldn't have had anything to worry about since Kraznik had signed the register in Vegas.

Hopefully, Tina would have something to tell Sam about a location and get him away from London.

****

Now in his hotel Maximilian Hohen-Zeitfest saw that Tina Kraznik had not only written, but had called. She had asked about him from the reception desk. He would have to do something; his mother was right, being seen with Tina Kraznik should not get into the papers again.

He would have to do something – she was going to become a problem if she was stalking him. He would think of something.

The result of his thinking was a decision to use the usual goodbye tactic. He would let her know he was only briefly in Paris – had a number of things that had to be done, but would like to have drinks. He would meet her somewhere and they could stop by somewhere for a cocktail. No dinner. She would understand that that was all there was going to be.

Well, to be fair, it was true that he was busy; for one thing, he had the automobile show. With this, a slight hint of interest seeped into his thinking. Kravonia had for some time been an excellent place for automobile manufacturers to have established plants – they had skilled labor and were close to the European markets. A number of companies had done this, but he had always felt there was more to be done with the automobile industry than this. As an amateur racer the subject interested him.

Chapter 5

The weather wasn't bad that year in France. Rain had alternated with heat, but not enough to upset the Tourist Bureau. There were more Algerian taxi drivers than ever, and every nationality was seen in the streets.

Flags flew constantly in the Place de la Concorde – a constant stream of dark skinned dignitaries from new nations filed through the Palais de l'Élysée. The French newspapers lambasted the world's youth, but especially that of England, who had led the way with the latest amplified music, turning the pop culture upside down and inspiring imitators in Holland and the United States. A Catholic newspaper headlined the French infection of the British pathology – exemplified by the same music.

The so-called provocateurs and juvenile drug addicts also passed in review, while French youth – poorer and twenty years more conservative than their Anglo-Saxon brothers – rioted over the mathematics exams set for the *bac.* This was a yearly protest – almost a tradition; then they rioted again in protest against the University facilities. Ministers debated the gaining drop-out rate among them.

Worker priests, a big item at the time, were in the news again, this time the subject of Labor Union propaganda, but the Yves postcards of the Paris landmarks sold by the thousands as usual.

Over the city, the spires of the Sainte Chapelle and Notre Dame continued their centuries-old dialogue, a dialogue from which such newcomers as the Tour Eiffel are forever excluded.

On rainy days the Arc de Triomphe stood solidly in the grey mist of rain and was painted by the artists who paint Paris under rain. On sunny days the Park Monceau, the Bois de Boulogne and the Gardens of the Rond Point could forget the present and dwell in an eternal world of Impressionist images.

Tourists filed into the Louvre by the thousands; they had just time to reach the Greek sculpture and 19th century paintings before the bell rang and they left, as had happened for generations.

In the kitchens of the restaurant, La Tour d'Ivoire, the chef sat holding a cigar with the owner, Jean Paul Sareil, and made up a menu that could be catered conveniently to the I Love Paris Ball in the old Hôtel Plessis. There were no kitchens in the Hôtel Plessis and not all the courses could be hot.

The two de la Rocque sisters and their mother did a little very cautious shopping. They had decided that, in fact, it would be better to find Beatrice a white dress for the I love Paris Ball, but there were also other things needed; they looked in the Gallerie Lafayette and Le Printemps as well as smaller boutiques. The girls knew that this France and its culture belonged to them, but it also felt a little alien. Having spent their lives in America and having a Bostonian mother they did not feel quite French. This happens to the French who live in Anglo-Saxon countries. They can never quite go home again.

Chong Sam, the white Pekinese, curled up and slept in an assortment of odd places – in hat check rooms of museums, under tea tables and beside park benches.

He was used to the sounds of Paris now. He had grown accustomed to sweeping up the leaves and cigarette ends of Paris in his luxuriant white fur; sniffing to the right and left with a sensitive nose which informed him of the passing of an occasional horse, donkey rides, exhaust and chestnut blossoms. His short-slighted eyes could see the reassuring ankles of Her and the other one; ankles that walked gracefully and firmly, talking, talking, sometimes saying things that interested him – words like "hungry," "stop," "be careful" and "cake"; she was his responsibility. Usually she brushed his fur but sometimes she had cried into it, and he knew that you have to lick human's faces if they do that. They stop immediately.

On the grand Boulevard Haussmann, the foreign automobile showrooms prepared a show of new small cars, timed to attract tourists in Paris. Australian students in France, studying at Oxford and Cambridge, sold the European editions of American newspapers on the

Champs Élysées and near the Opéra in Brooklynese accents learned from the movies.

Early in the morning fashion magazine photographers posed the latest looks for youth among the trucks and workmen of Les Halles. The models posed with bunches of vegetables, bales of cut flowers and crates of oysters.

Clarkson Finch filled in his days in Paris one way and another. He took his car to have its wheels aligned, which occupied the greater part of one day. He struggled to communicate with the mechanic, who was a stout man in greasy blue overalls whose favorite gesture was a hopeless, dubious, heaving shrug, which he performed with the whole of his immense body, much like a baby whale trying to breathe. He actually spoke excellent English, having been liaison to the British and the Resistance during the war, but he disliked Americans, so he did not understand.

Clarkson also bought postcards of Folies Bergère girls which he sent to everyone for whom he had an address in New York with little messages like "Paris is great," and "So what if Paris is expensive?" He and Alex did a few things together and Alex gave him Olivia Bryce-Smith's number at the Castelagni Fashion House. Alex didn't find her interesting, but gave Clarky to understand that she was pretty sharp.

For a couple of days Clarky went over to the Boul' Mich and sat in the Café Blum with Ivan but he was too innately sedate to like it. He didn't like to be there without Ivan. He grew his hair a little longer, but couldn't bring himself to be shaggy.

****

One of the reasons that French aristocrats are so difficult to find is that they eat at home. Even the English are surprised by how often the French eat at home, and how many are at home to eat at the same time.

In the avenue Matignon apartment of the Duke de Ruissy, for instance, not only the duke is there – home from whatever business he may have found to transact during the morning – but his mother is there to preside at table and his wife has come in from the various socio/charitable acts she does each day.

It has always been a little bit of a mystery to French husbands where their wives go every day. The duke's brother, Gérard, also eats lunch at the family apartment, but, of course, in his case it is less surprising because having no particular occupation he spends the mornings in the apartment anyway. At other times of year the children return from school for lunch before disappearing again until the end of the day.

In this case, however, the duke's younger children, still struggling with *le bac*, had finished the school year and gone to their maternal grandmother in the Sarthe.

His eldest son, Olivier, was also home. He was a quiet, loose-limbed young man with the family nose and sandy hair. He was amused by his family, having been out of the country long enough to see them, and their situation, somewhat disparagingly. He would be duke one day, but he was aware that making a living and knowing the world would be what he really needed. The responsibility of keeping the family property intact in the modern world was something he hated to think about and knew was in his future.

Gérard, meanwhile, was a popular man-about-town and just the evening before had been to the Feldenstein's gallery opening. He had accompanied Charlotte Schlemmer, who amused him, and whom he knew through his brother's position with Bilco Oil. She was grateful for his escort while her husband was still in Nantes and it did her social aspirations no harm.

The Feldensteins had prepared carefully for their regular June cocktail reception/exhibition. The show would include a number of Central European painters, of which Feldenstein senior was one of the first in the business to discover. It would also feature a number of late 18th century portraits, and the latest painting by the American artist Monty Flabster of an enormous banana.

Alex had slicked down his rather too curly hair, put on a red waistcoat, unearthed a cigarette holder, posed with this in a knowledgeable slouch in front of his full length mirror, and prepared to enjoy the gallery event.

He had suggested to his friend Clarky Finch, whom he ran into at the Bar Arizona in the rue St. Benoit, that he might get on over for it. It was sure to cause quite a stir; it would cause a stir because of the critics and writers his father had invited, and because of the quality of the champagne which ensured them all coming.

Alex enjoyed these evenings hugely. He imitated his father's manner of talking about the paintings and learned the names of all the guests – guests who drifted around the parquet floors with narrowed eyes, champagne in one hand, catalogues in the other.

The Feldenstein galleries were in one of the last great Hôtels particuliers on the Rue du Faubourg St. Honoré. The rooms, large and gracious, were designed with exquisite plaster work on the ceilings and marble fireplaces. The pictures were always spaced out and gracefully hung – as gracefully as one can hang central European paintings.

Once these rooms had belonged to the niece of Madame de Sévigné, at a time when the more conservative members of French society remained in the old section of Paris in the shadow of the Louvre. Here the *Opéra* was brought to perform at the desire of the young Prince de Condé a generation before the Revolution sent surviving members of the Royal Family into exile in England.

It had been a misty, dark blue night on the Rue du Faubourg when the *Opéra* performers came by torch-light for the young prince. Guests had arrived by carriages or carried in sedan chairs made of rosewood with marquetry and some inlaid with ivory. You can see some of them now on Second Avenue in New York, fitted up to be sideboys for china pieces. But the night that the *Opéra* came, dress-swords hung at the sides of small graceful gentlemen, who rubbed shoulders with gamblers and social climbers of the day. The opera had been haphazardly performed in the *grand salon*, but everyone enjoyed the ballet sequences. La Gigotte had danced. It was one of her last performances before she contracted small pox. All deserted her when she died except the old clown, to whom it turned out she had been married all along. Like the other great actress, Adrienne Lecouvreur, she could not be buried on sacred ground, but was thrown into a lime pit and, like Adrienne, she was admired by Voltaire. Her black eyes are immortalized in a painting known as *L'Opéra Comique* by an un-named painter of the time.

It is said that young Condé had been one of her lovers, which is why the *Opéra* came that night. They served ratafia – sweet wines and spiced cake with other delicacies of the period. It is all described in an anonymously published book titled, *Les Histoires et les On Dits des Escaliers de France*. It was whispered that night when the *Opéra* came that the Duchesse de la Paille left early and was delivered of a child at five in the morning at a nearby convent. The duke could never prove it, though he must have wondered. It was also said that here Madame de Lafayette had spent some painful weeks when her husband was first imprisoned; here that Tsar Alexander had held a meeting with the Prussian general Blücher after Napoleon's defeat at Leipzig.

Neither Charlotte Schlemmer nor Parisian art enthusiasts gave any thought to the history of the building that night. On this particular evening the Feldensteins had collected a crowd which included actual buyers; so often a party of this kind was only an occasion for half of Paris to have free champagne.

By the time Mrs. Schlemmer arrived with Gérard de Ruissy the rooms were already filled with people in the special kind of clothes worn on these occasions. Women usually felt the need to wear something that showed the mystic in them at concerts and gallery openings. They wore black or draped crepe, unusual hairdos and often wraps. Mrs. Schlemmer knew better than that and came in a tweed suit. It was not an ordinary tweed suit, of course; it was a Castamagni original with bright pink flecks and a chiffon blouse. Her bag and shoes were snakeskin – grey snakeskin – and she did not wear a hat. If it hadn't been for her gold charm bracelet, one would have supposed that she was French.

Among the people gathered there were the French singer, Armand Legosse, and a few members of diplomatic missions. There were several miscellaneous Baronesses – one Napoleonic, one counterfeit and one Belgian. There were a number of American collectors and some people from London galleries on Curzon Street.

Clarky Finch stood in one corner of the room where he was seen by the cousin of someone at the US Embassy.

"Clarky darling!, Hi there.. why don't you call us at the Crillon? I can't stand it, you men living it up in Paris and never looking up the people you know."

In another corner two men from London told each other that in an adjoining room there were some 18th century sketches of gardens that might be worth taking a second look at, which was what Mr. Feldenstein hoped they would think when he put them there.

Gérard de Ruissy enjoyed himself that evening – he was the centre of a small circle, as he usually was when among his social inferiors. He was being asked his opinion on the paintings. Even the French cannot believe that the brother of a duke is not a collector and connoisseur of objets d'art, of ballet dancers, and other such things equally expensive. He manages to encourage this feeling with those shrugs and pouts with which the French suggest they are suggesting so much and saying so little.

Before the evening was over, Alex and Clarky had joined the group talking with Gérard and Mrs. Schlemmer. Alex made a point of looking knowing and asking them how they liked the collections. He snapped his fingers for more champagne and put another cigarette into his holder. He introduced Clarky to Mrs. Schlemmer and Gérard, who affected a Charles Boyer manner when talking to young people, said, "No young girls for you boys here tonight, *hein*?" Clarky blushed.

"How do you find our Parisian girls, young American?"

"Pretty easily, I guess."

"For me," Gérard raised his glass, "I appreciate the women of your United States. What animal beauty – stature. We have not that kind of beauty here in France. *Chic*, yes, charm, perhaps, but beauty is rare. We admire even your Hollywood actresses."

This put Alex in mind of something. He asked Clarky, "How come you didn't get Tina along tonight?" This seemed unfair to Clarky. He shrugged, but smiled.

"Tina Kraznik," Alex – never loathe to name-drop if possible – explained to Gérard and Charlotte Schlemmer, "was Tina Vance."

"Ah?" Gérard didn't like Alex Feldenstein much.

"She's here to find a location to film *Les Cousines,* she told me. As a matter of fact they might use the Tourbonnière place. We talked about it."

This wasn't how Clarky remembered it.

"Tourbonnière?," Gérard was interested again. "Do you mean the de la Rocque Tourbonnière family? I believe they are in America."

Charlotte said, "I don't know about that, but there is a Tourbonnière girl to be presented at the ball that Bilco Oil is sponsoring."

Gérard gave his elegant shrug.

****

Luncheon is served in the Ruissy apartment by a Spanish girl with as much formality as she can be got to understand. The day in question, which was Wednesday, she served radishes as a first course. Gérard de Ruissy put butter on a radish and smiled to himself. He was delighted to have something to tell his sister-in-law that she didn't already know.

It was the day after the Feldenstein's show; he said, casually, that it was interesting about the Tourbonnière girls.

"What is interesting, Gérard?"

"About the film."

"About what film?"

"Hadn't you heard?"

"Heard what?"

"I thought you said something about it the other night."

"About what, for the love of God?"

"No, you are right. It was Charlotte."

"Charlotte? What does she know about les Tourbonnières?"

"No, I remember now. It was at the Feldenstein Gallery. Charlotte hadn't heard about it either."

"Are the Tourbonière girls in films? I thought they were débutantes, coming for the ball."

"*Mais non*, Henriette. Not exactly in films."

"Gérard," said his mother, "stop teasing Henriette."

"I do not tease, Maman. I wish to be exact. Truth lies in exactitude. Yes, the Tourbonnières are arranging for the château de la Tourbonnière to be used as a location for a film."

"*Pas possible!*"

"I suppose that is why they are in France."

"But the château belongs to the old lady."

"I suppose that our cousin has arranged it – do you have any idea of what they must pay?"

"It is probably extraordinary, *Chérie,*" said the young duchess to her husband.

"Do you hear? But that is extraordinary. Why do not we do that with Ruissy? Why did we not think of that – think of the money! And Ruissy is much better, much bigger, much older, altogether better in every way. *Chérie*, we should arrange for Ruissy to be used as a film location."

The Ruissy family, much as they would have liked not to be constantly concerned about paying for things, had always felt that Henriette's concern with money was a sign that her family was not as old as theirs and betrayed evidence of some past admixture with the bourgeoisie, and it had always made them uncomfortable.

"It depends on the film, after all. Toubonnière and Ruissy are not at all alike. Tell, Gérard, what is the film?" asked the older duchess.

Her daughter-in-law broke in, "That makes no difference, *ma mère*, everyone knows that they change what they wish in a film. To a producer from Hollywood Ruissy would seem altogether better in every way."

"It seems," Gérard buttered his last radish, "that it is a film version of *Les Cousines*."

"But that is horrible!" His sister-in-law was incensed. "It was written by a Freemason. It is a disgusting story. How much, Gérard, did they say that they pay for such a location?"

"I have no idea."

"I will find out. We could keep Bellefontaine. It would be an advertisement unimaginable for the guided tours. *Chérie,* do you not see?

The tourists would pay double to see where a star has been – double, I am sure, than to see where a queen was poisoned."

"My dear wife, it could perhaps be interesting, but we can hardly wish to take from the Tourbonnières something they have arranged to their advantage, Also, it is an old manor; Ruissy is a medieval castle. They may not have any need for a set such as Ruissy."

"*Pouf*! I have already explained that. It needs only that Madame your mother invite the producer to tea and *pan*,' it is done. They are snobs these people. You will see."

"We will not try to take this arrangement from the Tourbonnière family."

Henriette de Ruissy could not understand the way her family passed up opportunities. What was wrong with Gérard, for instance, that he didn't find out more about these people looking for a location in Normandy? She herself would have immediately found out all about it. She would much rather get the château used as a location than rent it – or whatever they would be forced to do next. With the money Hollywood tossed around!

She thought on: Americans spend millions on things like that it was well known! They were forced to open Ruissy to the public anyway in order to collect help from the government – but if it were used in a film then they would get people from everywhere and charge more for the tour and do it properly. What advertising a film would be! Certainly *Les Cousines* was a horrible book; well, frankly, she hadn't read it, but everybody knew it was a horrible book written by someone odious, socialist, very *mal pensant* and everyone said a Freemason, but everyone knew they change everything in the movies, so what difference did it make?

She had always felt that her family had never taken advantage of situations. Gérard, for instance: why hadn't he married that widow? She had money, that one, and wasn't so bad. And then Hervé, with his position, and with his connection with Bilco Oil – he had not thought of working out more to their advantage with the Historic Monuments commission – and now it was Charlotte who had made an arrangement with that Egyptian for the I Love Paris Ball! Men!

Ever since her aunt de Monfusil had suggested Hervé to her as a possible husband, it had been she, Henriette, who had made all the decisions. She had fought with her father until he agreed to put out the funds in her name, a *dot*, that would make the marriage possible. Her mother-in-law had never quite liked her, but the dowager duchess was a Combrousse d'Halaine, and that was a family that thought itself above everyone. They were a family that had as many priests as titled relatives, and as many saints in their family tree as royal names. Even in Italy few families can boast of that.

The senior duchess' family came from the Château des Fantes in the southwest. It annoyed Henriette that it was an historic fortress and still unopened to the public, although, agreed, it was in deplorable condition. Her mother-in-law's family considered themselves *des grands seigneurs de province* and had never stooped to becoming courtiers or politicians.

The younger duchess' family had, in fact, increased their fortunes many times by hanging around at Versailles. They were *nobles de cour*, rather than *nobles de robe*. Henriette felt that since it was such a long time ago, little dishonour was attached to their having certain estates granted through the influence of Madame de Montespan, but you know what it is! People allied to the Cambrouse d'Halaine family would feel superior forever.

Her husband's family, the Ruissys, had also been one of the great provincial powers, but they, at least, had been involved with the central seats of power, and she could not understand their present day unworldliness.

The older duchess looked up, having supervised the serving of the second course.

"This is all a lot of nonsense," she said, "I do not know how you can have made all these ideas. The younger de la Rocque daughter is to be presented at the ball Mrs. Schlemmer is organizing for the benefit of the Historic Monuments – that is all. I have been asked to find some young men to invite. That is all that is happening."

Nevertheless late that afternoon the younger duchess of Ruissy played bridge with a group that included the American ambassadress and she explained in excellent English, learned from a governess as child, that obviously she could leave very little to her mother-in-law, who was undoubtedly a sainted woman, or to her husband – men can never really manage.

She really had to attend to many things herself – you know what it is – now the children were away she had so much to do to help her mother-in-law, who was patroness of the I Love Paris Ball – to which she understood the Ambassadress had agreed to attend. Further, she added, they were considering allowing Hollywood to use the Château de Ruissy as a location for a film. But everything was left to her.

Henriette did not know she was lying, but felt it was true when she said it.

Chapter 6

The drinks party planned by Mrs. Payne Glenn at the Ritz was scheduled for two days after this.

The day was spent in various ways by those who planned to attend it. The de la Rocque sisters took the dog to the park with their mother. It seemed to them that Ivan's party was just more New York, and it did not concern them much.

Ivan himself, who would be the host at this affair, spent some time at a film festival on the Left Bank by himself, and Clarkson Finch tried to explain to the mechanic that he thought the left front wheel of his car still needed aligning.

Tina had gone out the night before with some of Sam's friends, but she had started worrying again. She worried about Sam and waited for Max to call – it had given her a nervous stomach.

Now there's one thing you can say for Sam Kraznik as a husband – his wives have all found him very open-handed. It is part of his idea of status that his wife should have a generous amount of spending money. When they go to Miami Beach, he likes to see that they have the best rooms in the biggest hotels. He likes to see his wives in the latest cut of the latest fur (people still wore furs in those days). As an ex-husband, however, not quite so much can be said. He gave the wife before Tina quite a big settlement, but then she was his favorite, and she had also had a child.

Tina only knew of one way to calm anxiety – shopping, and to a lesser degree meeting for gossip with a girl friend. She decided on both of these. As she had money now she would go out and see what was out there. She would also call a starlet just arrived in town who she knew slightly, and meet with her for coffee.

She put on her white Castamagni suit and a silk turban, and met for coffee at an outdoor table at the Regalis Plaza with Lea Bartlett. Lea

Bartlett had just arrived from California to do a show. She sat near a profusion of geraniums such as is seen on magazine covers and in Paris, but rarely in real life.

Tina felt better talking with Lea about Hollywood gossip, and who was in Vegas, and who was out of work. She sat in the sunshine telling her about her love life and the clothes she was having made. She told Lea that there were some cute men around and hinted that there was a big possibility in her future. By the time she finished hinting about Max she nearly believed it all herself – just as Henriette de Ruissy believed her own story. Lea was an avid listener and was always thrilled for her friends if they got a break.

After her coffee with Lea, she went and bought ten pairs of shoes. It made her feel much better. The attitude of the saleswoman buoyed her up, the beauty of her feet in the shoes gave her back some of her old assured glide. Shopping made her feel part of the world again; a happy member of the throng, one of the people on the sidewalks who had a reason to be there. And there is something exhilarating about waving down a taxi when one's arms are full of packages. How often in New York she had posed – mouth slightly open, joy in her bearing – in front of cardboard reproductions of the Tour Eiffel, or one of the cameramen dressed up as a Paris *flic* – but this was the real thing: it was Tina's idea of Paris. She hummed *The Last Time I saw Paris* to herself.

When she returned to the hotel she felt better than she had for days. She decided to have lunch by herself somewhere – somewhere where she would be on show – it would be a shame to waste all the time it had taken to get dressed. She chose to go to Fouquets; to wear dark glasses and look beautiful – mysterious – and order champagne. She was a wonderful advertisement for the clothes she wore.

Ari would be back tomorrow; Buddy was going to help her. This evening she would see if she could find out what the score was on the castle in Normandy, or wherever it was, and she had a date with Max. Hell, if she could get Sam back for the rest of the summer, who knew what she might not be able to fix up. She might need those dresses for Africa after all.

Tina's idea of Africa was lifted directly from movies made from novels by Hemingway, and everyone knows that if you go to Africa and wear a pith helmet, you will also meet someone that looked liked Stewart Granger – and who needs Sam in that case? She had heard a lot about men in Africa.

She felt much better by the end of all this, but the champagne made her sleepy. What she needed was a nap and a couple of hours to get ready for the evening.

Maximilian had spent the morning at the automobile show. He looked seriously at all the latest models – allowed himself to be led from one car to another, thinking nostalgically about the Ferrari he had driven in the 24 Hours some years before. He had stood with his hands clasped behind his back – as Princes do who have done their stint in the Royal Navy – and remembered people's names. He was gracious enough and he had smiled to himself that his mother would be pleased. He had stood at the podium and said a few words and snipped a red ribbon. He had shaken hands with automobile manufacturers and garage owners – although truth to tell, the ones he enjoyed speaking with were the mechanics. He had spoken about the place of his country in the automobile industry, even though he knew it would take real work to make such a thing a reality.

In the back of his mind there was still a polo field, a boat, any number of things, but as he spoke he had a nascent feeling that it might be interesting to do something with the automobile industry.

Maximilian returned to his room in a depressed state of mind; he would have to do something about Tina – the note and the calls had begun to look to him like stalking. He frowned – perhaps he would be less concerned if he had not got that letter from his mother.

Although he hadn't decided on how to block her calls and he did not want to see her, Tina's almost innocent lowness would have amused him if he weren't now really annoyed. In Europe, he thought, sluts know they are sluts; Tina didn't seem to know any such a thing. Maximilian did not know the United States well enough to know whether this was her own personal brand, or whether it was part of American culture. He thought that probably in America people with Tina's morals fell under the heading of being allowed to have one's own point of view.

So it was that Maximilian reluctantly put a call through to Tina with the plan he had in mind. He would suggest drinks, no dinner, make it short, and she would understand that there was going to be no more to it.

Tina got Maximilian's call to her immense relief. Her heart beat a little faster when he asked where they could meet. Thinking quickly she suggested, "I have to be at a cocktail at the Ritz tonight. I'm seeing some people about a location for Sam. Sam's in London. Why don't we meet in the lobby at 8:30? It would be great to catch up. I thought maybe you had forgotten me."

She couldn't see Maximilian shake his head in disbelief and amusement at the frankness of her approach. Probably his grandfather King Albert II had the same feeling about the more-than-frank approach of Nellie, the dancer from the Royal Opera. It was so amusing that she didn't seem to realize who or what she was. He forgot momentarily that he, too, frequently forgot who and what he was.

As he agreed to this she thought, so it might all be fine. When you're down there's nowhere to go but up. Drinks at the Ritz, and maybe she would straighten things out with Sam for a little longer – a date with Max, and Buddy thought that a date with royalty could be a back-up. He was only some kind of Prince, but it gave her a thrill to think of herself as almost a King's mistress. How high could you go? They had only a casual acquaintance in Torremolinos, just one of those holiday things, but it could get better. She had heard of Kings' mistresses who had fantastic jewelry. Hell!, stranger things had happened.

She looked marvelous that night.

****

The two de la Rocque sisters also prepared for cocktails at the Ritz. They would take a taxi – their mother having decided to spend the evening with their aunt; they were, after all, invited by their young New York friends, she had said. They had begun to see that it would take some effort – perhaps only when their father came – for them to meet any French friends. This party they were going to was just more of their New York experience.

Madame de Lespinasse was also concerned that they were meeting no young Frenchmen; she worried as she heard their footsteps in the courtyard.

After half century in her apartment on the rue de la Boétie, she had developed a sixth sense about those who walked through the courtyard and why. She could tell the age and businesses of all the voices she heard, and their state of mind. And although she could not tell her grandsons anything about their gearshift or the make of their car, she knew each of the cars housed in the courtyard by the sound of its engine. She could tell who was driving it by the number of times the accelerator was gunned, as it turned in the drive, and whether the driver was happy or sad.

Madame de Lespinasse was not a busybody; her motives were purely benevolent, and she never showed by the slightest trace of an expression that she knew these things.

The French have made community living possible by a common agreement to be dishonest about personal feelings. In most cases they simply do not show them at all, and if they do, one has a right to ignore them.

In the few weeks that the de la Rocque girls had been living at No. 39 she had learned the sound of their heels and the light tones of their voices. She worried about them and hoped that God had seen fit to allow her to help them. She wondered now where they were going. She knew they had met American friends, and, after all, their mother – no doubt a women of merit – was nevertheless American.

At a second floor widow, one of the du Buisson Fleuri boys called to his brothers to look at the de la Rocque girls going out.

"They go to a cocktail," said the knowledgeable one.

"How that is American," said the sulky one.

"Not at all," said the one that wanted to be a priest. "A great many people go to cocktails. Maman went to one, I remember, last year."

"But not the young."

"If one is invited, there is no harm in going."

"They must have a lot of money," said the sulky one.

"And so? I would like to have it, too," said the one who wanted to be a priest.

"They are very pretty, our cousins."

"Oh, it is a type."

"Well it is a pretty type."

"For me," said the knowledgeable one, "I do not think they have so much money. They would have rented a car."

"I would not like America," said the sulky one.

"What do you know about it?," asked the future priest. "America is a magnificent country – they have everything: mountains, skyscrapers, highways."

"France is better."

"What do you know about it? Think of the automobiles in America. Everyone has three or four."

"What ? Everyone?"

"Yes, stupid. Everyone knows that. Three or four big cars for everyone. It is necessary – the country is so big."

"Beatrice is very beautiful," said the knowing one.

"Oh," said the sulky one, "You say that because she has yellow hair. The other one has spirit."

"I like them both," said the future priest. "They promised to send me stamps from America for my collection."

****

Eleanor Payne Glenn did not know exactly who was coming to her cocktail, but she always had these rooms. The rooms overlooked the Place Vendôme, that now, at 7 in the evening, was growing dark. In the evening there are parts of Paris that take on thoughts of their own – they turn inward and exist for themselves. At those moments and in these places, the fashionable, the tourists, the sightseers, become meaningless. The cobbles are remembering their early years under the lost statue of Louis le Grand, the iron hoofs that bound the wheels of phaetons, perhaps even the distant rumble of tumbrils. The buildings seem to commune with something past, with sounds one simply cannot hear. Ghosts are seen at times like that.

The Place Vendôme is not very old – not by French standards, as it dates only from 1698 – but even here it has memories of people it prefers to the traffic and the vulgarity of a modern summer. Its proportions were planned for horse-drawn traffic, and the lines of its buildings to harmonize with a different style of dress. It had endured through many generations. Chopin lived there.

Eleanor Payne Glenn assumed she would know her guests when they came. There were friends she always looked up and some people Ivan knew. There were some people who had come over on the ship with her and John and Pauly. She always saw John and Pauly in Europe – they were so amusing.

John Trent was someone normally seen in the Ritz and its equivalents with Pauly, for whom he paid all expenses. This relationship had long been accepted as not only inevitable but charming by those Americans who return annually to Europe and to their preferred hotel and want to go to a party – by women whose husbands want to sit in the hotel lobby and smoke a cigar and do not know which restaurant to go to, or how to order wine.

John Trent entertained intimately and extravagantly in balconied suites from New York to Istanbul – in fact, in whichever part of Europe he felt had not been discovered by philistines. His guests were usually titled, elderly women, perhaps a minor opera star, and anyone who knows about Art with a capital A. He is an authority on where to obtain the best of anything and can be seen at first nights in any number of opera houses, although he is not likely to stay for the third act.

John Trent verged on corpulence; he had shining – suspiciously shining – golden hair and polished finger nails. His eyes were an angelic blue and he spoke in a tone of blasé complaint, delivered in the manner of a disappointed child. He and Pauly had already arrived when the garçon from downstairs opened the door to Francesca and Beatrice. John Trent and Pauly always say that they noticed them immediately; "Well, I mean," they go on, "they were simply different – I mean, you could sense their quality right away, you really could."

Actually, when the de la Rocque girls arrived the room was a blur of colors with the sound of conversation buzzing. John Trent was complaining to someone called Edwina Flauthauser that no one knew their trade any more these days, not even jewellers – just that afternoon Pauly had to go down to Maubusson to return some gold cuff-links that weren't heavy enough.

I was there making notes for my column and noticed, as I had when we took the picture of Beatrice for the magazine, that Francesca seemed the more observant or engaged of the two – we had heard she was applying to law school and was clever – but the younger had a manner that suggested she would let the world go on around her without actually touching her.

John Trent and Pauly murmured that Beatrice looked interesting – a beautiful girl, but something removed about her. She just doesn't seem to belong to this world.

At this point, Tina made a sensational entrance looking stunning in another Castamagni design. She caught all of our attention. I was sorry not to have my cameraman with me. She would have brightened my *Where Are They Now?* article that week. She was wearing a slim black skirt with a white waistcoat jacket, spike heels and a small hat with a two-foot feather through it. Her looks, her clothes, her reputation gave her a starring role that one looked for in the much pictured models of the time.

None of the other women in the room could compare with her stylish presence and no one would notice that she had nothing to say, and no one knew she had no confidence at all. The English girl Olivia Bryce-Smith was wearing the newest thing from London – a silver sheath that hardly reached below her derrière. She had come in laughing, making a group with Ivan Nevsky and Clarky.

Beside these two everyone seemed dowdy.

Alex Feldenstein slid up to Tina as she came in, very much as if he were the host. He nearly snapped his fingers for the waiter to bring her champagne. He gave the impression that it was he, rather than Ivan, whose party it was, and asked her if there was anyone she wanted to meet, or knew.

Tina coming alone was actually grateful for this and said, in the soft voice she had learnt in Hollywood, that she saw the girls he had brought over to her hotel.

"Hi there," she said, "How've you bin?" After the obvious small talk she went on, "You know, I wanted to ask you about your aunt's castle. Sam, my husband, called and he's serious about finding a location for some scenes in his next picture. He'd be interested in seeing your aunt's place. He'll be coming to Paris; maybe he could call you, or your aunt."

It was Francesca who answered:

"We don't know anything about anything like that, but our father is coming to Paris this coming week for my sister's deb party. Maybe your husband should speak with him."

Tina's spirits rose. Maybe this was really something she could suggest to Sam.

"Good idea. Maybe you should let me have a number he could call."

When numbers had been exchanged Tina said, "So what have you been up to?"

Francesca answered, "We've been looking for a dress for my sister. You know she's supposed to come out at the American deb ball."

Then, with a surprising moment of sympathy, and perhaps gratitude, Tina said to Beatrice, "So you're coming out, is that right? You don't have your dress?"

"We're still looking," said Francesca.

"I'll tell you what, "said Tina. "I'll tell you what…go round to Castamagni – tell them I sent you. They have a back room with discounts on dresses that've been used on the runway. Your sister is tall, she might find something. Try it. Tell them I sent you."

This would actually happen, and to be fair, her gesture was not only part of a pact she hoped she was creating with them over the use of the tower, part of her effort to get Sam to France, but an actual act of sympathy for a fellow female looking for a dress. It was something she understood.

As John Trent listened in on this exchange, he said, "Just everybody is having their place used as a location nowadays. Where's your castle?"

"Oh, no, it's just a very old country house belonging to an aunt. It's just that it has a very old tower at the back. Just like something out of a fairy tale. All covered with ivy, but it is quite empty except for its turning stair."

"I love it," said Pauly. "It makes me feel that we could go right back in time. So romantic!"

The party moved on. At eight-thirty, like Cinderella, Tina gave a little gasp and said she had to be going. Others were leaving and the girls, grateful for the hint about the designer dress, went toward the elevator with Tina and John and Pauly. They joined them in saying goodbye to Mrs. Payne Glenn, who looked puzzled by the de la Rocque girls, paid no attention to Tina, but told John and Pauly to come back and have lunch another day.

Downstairs at 8:30 Maximilian of Hohen-Zeitfest leaned against a pillar behind an issue of the *Figaro* and waited for Tina. Few people ever recognized him if he didn't want them to. For one thing, one did not see minor royalty on television often and the many other celebrities were easier to recognize; also the Ritz was used to Maximilian and let him alone.

He was still angry with himself and with his life, and this extended to Tina as well, as he flipped through the pages of the newspaper.

The elevator came down somewhat crowded with the de la Rocques, John Trent, Pauly and Tina. As they rode down Pauly was talking about an opera, "I mean I could never say it was good, I mean, it was weally bad, actually. As a matter of fact I've never seen anything like it. A shame, weally when you think what the pwoduction must have cost. Such a shame a big contrast to Maria Carlotti! The sopwano must have weighed in at three hundred pounds. I said to John, I really did, that I could really see the stage bending under her. You know, I really could. And her voice... talk about a lion roaring but out came a mouse." No one paid any attention.

As the doors opened Tina said, "I'll be seeing you then," and moved across to the floor toward Maximilian, who looked up with a startled expression.

It was an odd look. He looked stunned. He looked like a man who had suddenly had an idea – a shock – an extraordinary idea, miraculous in its simplicity.

He stared over the top of his newspaper, a man struck speechless by the amazing clarity of what he had just understood. You see, Maximilian had just seen Beatrice.

How and why he reacted so violently to seeing her was something that he only sensed and never understood.

In fact, it wasn't so amazing. In the far reaches of forgotten but seminal memories was the seventeen year-old nursery-maid in the Residence in Peltz who, thirty-five years before, had cared for him as a very young boy. A face as beautiful and calm – one which looked at him in a way no one else had ever done – true and caring, as well as beautiful. It had been his introduction to life and the realization that someone could make sense of things, a feeling he had not found since.

He saw that face now with its expression of calm. It was the missing piece of the puzzle suddenly found. Maximilian's life didn't make perfect sense in that moment, but he knew that it was about to do so.

"Well, hello," said Tina.

"Excuse me, Tina. Who was that girl?"

"Which girl?"

"The girl in the elevator with you."

"There were two of them. Well, three, if you count Pauly."

"That one there."

"Come *on*, Max! She's some kind of debutante."

He heard them say, "Shall we call a taxi?" And the sister say, "No, no, let's walk," and they disappeared into the dark.

"But who is she?"

"You're very curious all of a sudden."

Tina did not feel her date with Maximilian was starting well.

****

As they reached their apartment Beatrice said, “Who do you think that man was?”

“What man?”

“Didn’t you see?”

“No, what man?”

“The man in the Ritz.”

“I can’t imagine.”

In Beatrice’s mind he would always be the man in the Ritz.

Chapter 7

In the moment that Maximilian stared over the top of his newspaper, it occurred to him with undeniable logic for the first time in his adult life that he was grateful for his position. Now that he saw her it was obvious why his life had seemed arid, ugly, empty. Here it was – the charm, the beauty, the comfort that he had been looking for since when, at three years old, Fraulein Schelling had been become his nursery-maid.

He was stunned by a sense of something like *déjà vu* he couldn't explain. Rather than just for a cocktail, however, he took Tina to the Langouste Dorée, a restaurant so "in" that the *Guide Michelin* had to beg to mention it, and eventually with some clever conversational manipulation got Tina to tell him that the girl was called Beatrice de something with a place called Tourbonnière, if she was pronouncing it correctly, and that she and Sam were thinking of using it as a location.

That explained to Maximilian the otherwise inexplicable fact of Tina being in the same universe with this vision. He had no intention of asking Tina to introduce them, however. Having at least part of her name, he would find out the rest and get her invited to one of the embassy events or ask some of his French friends to do it, the Hermous d'Offrance family, perhaps, they might know them. He took Tina home early and did not say when he might call again.

Tina was not happy at all. She was enraged. She knew exactly what that treatment meant. It meant he was dumping her. She had been anxious and depressed all week and now this jerk had the nerve to leave her like that at the door of the hotel, and ask her about some little girl half his age.

Tina felt as if she would like to get even. She had counted on being seen with him on Buddy's advice. The trouble with the royalty she had met since her marriage to Sam, which included someone called Fakim, who didn't seem to be European, and Princess Saradera – she wasn't sure she was European either – was that every now and then they clammed up and looked through you – and you never quite knew when it was going to happen. Now Maximilian had done it. Who the Hell did he think he was?

From the Eden Roc to Hollywood, from the yacht club at Lyford Cay to Athens, Tina held on to Sam's world by her false eyelashes, by looking perfect in a black and white bikini – by staying quiet and beautiful in turban hats and scarlet fingernails. She could stroll with model's ease through all those places and she could always adopt the assurance of the clothes she wore, but she knew that at the end of the trail, even for the successful girls, lay at best a one-story home in Beverly Hills or Santa Barbara; for the unsuccessful there would only be calendar shots, as long as one's figure held out, or marriage to a restaurant owner in Ventura. In Tina's world one became a has-been so abruptly and so completely that a void encircled anyone who did not have funds of their own.

Tina knew her career was a washout; that in New York and Hollywood she was now known chiefly as Sam's wife.

It was funny, though, she thought, what a foul humour Max had been in. When she had met him in Torremolinos it had been different. He had been different there – relaxed. He had been with Bobo and Larry, heir to the marquis of Longfray, when they had stopped on a yacht borrowed from Fakim.

That Maximilian did go on jaunts of that kind had been the plague of Queen Helen's life. At eighteen it was obvious to his tutors, his uncles, his father and his advisors, that he was a headstrong, clever, rebellious boy – an inconvenience to a royal house in any period. He was taller and quicker than Peter. In the Middle Ages they would have sent him to invade somewhere – simply to get him away from court, where he would have made trouble for entrenched ministers, and gone wenching. At a later date he would have been a liberal and founded rival factions to the throne.

As it was, he had done well at University and during his five years with their cousin's Royal Navy, but in a restless sort of way. He had thrown himself into all the most dangerous sports. He flew and skydived with the King of Jordan; sent on official visits he shot tigers without the proper precautions. With the President of the United States he went deep sea fishing until the State Department put the boat out of commission. He played polo at Windsor, of course, where he broke a collar bone. He threatened to race at Le Mans, the year there were five deaths.

Peter had tried to make him an advisor to keep him within the national interest, but he had too many opinions, and lost interest when he saw there was nothing he could really say or do that would be adopted.

Since Peter's marriage he had seen less and less of him, anyway. Peter had become depressingly domestic and was always wearing one of fifty uniforms for one function or another.

Maximilian was a misfit and Queen Helen wondered whether it would have been better had he been a girl. His friends were a disaster, and through his racing he knew every mechanic who knew his job from Scotland to Prague; he was always to be found having a beer with them and was photographed doing anything. It looked very bad.

Actually, Parliament granted him only a nominal income and his money came from his maternal grandmother, but the people didn't know that. It was wrong, anyway, for him to do nothing – such a waste!

During the years in the Royal Navy he had been part of English society and had got a taste for London, where he was seen in nightclubs and gambling casinos. He had made friends with Larry Langfrey, as the marquis was known – one of the aristocrats no longer welcome at Windsor, having been embroiled in scandal and married a twice-divorced model. Max insisted on seeing some of his friends even while they were being dragged across the broadsheets for some scandal or legal case, and even shooting grouse with them in Scotland during the hearings.

In Germany, where they had many, many relatives he spent months with people who were known to have – well, were thought to have – behaved badly during the war. Some of these, it seemed to her, were loose, bad mannered, and politically compromised, even arms profiteers, perhaps. He was often silent and moody and wasn't always a good guest. His hosts were glad to have him for snobbish reasons, and some really liked him, but they always had the feeling that he just thought of them as a way to kill time. He gave the impression he was waiting for something.

Maximilian was Queen Helen's favorite son – that sort of man always is – but she dreaded the day when he would be greying and bitter; just another minor royal looking degraded at St. Moritz.

She had just heard from their embassy in Paris that his presence at the automobile show had been very good, but they regretted they could not report on the Prince's health as they had not seen him since his arrival in Paris.

But Queen Helen had no inkling of the idea that had just taken hold of his mind. He had always known, he told himself, that Kravonia was the right place to develop an automobile industry. Not just a partner to German cars, which could be assembled there, but their very own mark. The country should begin by producing two models – a small two-horsepower car like the Renault *Deux Chevaux* and the VW Beetle for those just beginning to rise in the post-war period, and a super model – a car that could justly rival Porsche and Mercedes in style and innovations, a car that would put Kravonia on the map.

This, he now realized, was what he wanted to do. He would be happy to go home, create his own branch of the family and work this into something outstanding. He could do this in Peltz, but it suddenly occurred to him that the wooded mountains and winding valleys of Kravonia were the most beautiful he had ever seen, and why not build a really beautiful modern house overlooking one of their still lakes? Why had he never thought of that before?

The First Secretary at the Embassy looked up from his desk to see the small racing green sports-car driven by his Excellency Prince Maximilian, grand duke of the realm, turn into the courtyard.

The First Secretary had a long, sallow face and was dyspeptic. He was an odd sort of man – his brother and he had both grown up poor in a family that had fallen on hard times. The family circumstances had affected them differently. His brother had become one of the country's leading communist activists and backroom boys, whereas the First Secretary had become a cynical civil servant. The same frustration and love of power had made one a rebel and the other a discontented bureaucrat. In the case of the Embassy Secretary, however, the have-not and the secure bureaucrat warred within him and made him bitter.

He watched Prince Maximilian leave his car parked in front of the main entrance where it said, "No parking." He watched him come up the shallow steps four-at-a-time and supposed he would want something done in a hurry – his car shipped to Ischia, or hotel reservations somewhere impossible. The First Secretary knew a great deal about Prince Maximilian – more than Max would have dreamed possible. In fact, for some time past the secretary had kept a very full dossier on the Prince. The have-not within him knew there were some pretty ambitious men with whom his brother worked, who might use some of the information in his file if the time was right.

Maximilian came into his office without knocking and said good morning in the wrong language. In France he always spoke in French; then he said, without first showing that he remembered the First Secretary's name, that he wanted the address of a family by the name of Tourbonnière – they were not in the telephone directory. Would the secretary have someone check them out in the *Bottin Mondain* or the *Noblesse de France*?

To be clear, the *Bottin Mondain* is the French equivalent of the *Social Register* of New York; it is a large red volume in which most people of note could and can be found. The *Noblesse de France* is more restrictive than the *Bottin Mondain* as it lists the names of those families who were nobles before the French Revolution, many of whom have descendants reduced to a somewhat marginalized position in modern France, such as the Ruissy family.

By the way he gave the commission to his Under Secretary the First Secretary indicated that he had better things to do than look up the addresses of people he suspected were young women for a bachelor prince.

Maximilian didn't stay much longer than that in the Embassy office. He responded more or less graciously to the salutations of the little men in charcoal grey suits that called him "Your Excellency" and said the right things – but there was just too much naval commander left in Maximilian's manner to make him popular.

It was obvious to his people here at the Embassy that Maximilian had never enjoyed his official tasks and had a way of asking awkward questions when he went to open new dams, bridges or industrial plants for his brother. He had a reputation for being cutting and for preferring dangerous sports to the work his country asked of him. His suits, like his cars, were made in Italy or London – which annoyed his country's press. He did not seem to have the knack of being modern royalty; nor did he look like the bearded grandparents and great uncles, whose portraits lined the embassy walls wearing tight scarlet uniforms and peremptory mustaches.

The underlings of his embassy were drab and small, typical of the clerkly class of a modern socialist state. As in many socialist countries that have retained a royal family, their feelings toward them were ambivalent and ambiguous. These students of the common market and Swiss banks loved their king for the color he gave their lives and felt they ought to despise his brother for his playboy propensities.

King Peter's life is an open book, literally – anyone can buy the book for his coffee table. It is slick and full of color photographs showing Peter at his desk, Peter with his children, Peter playing golf with his wife, Peter riding his bicycle from the Summer Palace to the office, his wife's pregnancies, his birthday, his childhood memories – these are all in the possessions of his people.

The tough little figure of Max in the photographs of his early childhood had become a man who was hard to know and the people reserved judgment.

Peter had conveniently fallen in love with the first cousin of an acceptable branch of the family, a charming, somewhat self-effacing lady who was affectionately referred to as Queen Celestine, but Max, after offending all the fathers of suitable princesses in Europe, had married no one and was known to be seen with a very fast crowd. This was an offence to the Protestant population and an insult to the more patrician Roman Catholic families, whose daughters he had also overlooked.

A day later, after his visit to the Embassy, Maximilian got a call from the First Secretary.

"What do you mean? It can't be that hard to find these people. Gone to America? That's absurd. I saw her myself last week."

Just as I thought, said the First Secretary to himself, it's a girl he is looking for.

Maximilian did not want to telephone Tina to ask her more pointedly where he could find Beatrice; still, it looked as if there was nothing else for it. He had wanted to be able to meet this lovely girl formally, officially, in a way that would give rise to no gossip at all. The last thing he wanted to do was to drag Tina into it, or to seem to be trying to pick up someone who should be treated with dignity. After all, he thought, this is my future wife.

He wasn't going to wait any longer, however. In three weeks time he had agreed to represent his brother in Greece at an official family ceremony – the christening of a baby niece. Maximilian was sorry that he was not already married. She could have stood godmother to the baby princess in his stead. He imagined how well she would do it with her slender dignity and calm Madonna-like face, and she might have enjoyed it.

Maximilian was honest enough to realize he was almost enjoying himself. It made his him feel really young again to be ferreting out an unsuspecting girl in Paris. It was the first time he had had to go to some kind of effort to get hold of a girl since his eighteenth year when he had developed a passion for the wife of his mother's senior equerry. It was like a hunt – stalking dear like King Capethua. He really felt quite exhilarated and it was pleasant to be having an adventure that was blameless too.

He had smiled a little ruefully as he shaved for the evening – maybe this was what people called "Love at First Sight" and "Settling Down"; he had never expected either to happen to him. But now he did not question that they had, indeed, happened to him, and he now understood his life and his future.

He was putting on his black tie for a dinner with a Brazilian expatriate financier when a second call came from the Embassy, a call which told him that the de la Rocque Tourbonnière name was listed in the *Noblesse de France*, but that the family now lived in the United States.

His collar stud flew under the bed. Damn it. They were in France. He had seen her in the Ritz lobby.

A day later as they lay in their beds Beatrice said to Francesca. “Fran, who do you suppose that man was?”

“What man?”

“The one in the Ritz.”

Beatrice thought the whole thing of being a debutante at the Bilco Oil party was pleasant enough, and she was happy to go along with it. It had given her sister and her mother a lot of pleasure to go round with her to Castamagni and see all the wonderful discounted dresses, and she really liked the one they had chosen. But she really didn’t care about it that much.

Above all she was sick of these stupid young men. How boring. Why were none of them grown up?

A few days later Maximilian decided there was nothing for it but to get the whereabouts of the de la Rocques out of Tina somehow.

He decided on an approach. He would tell her that his mother was coming to Paris (which was true), and that she was planning to give a small reception for a cousin and their daughters and she had asked him to find some suitable guests (which was, of course, a complete lie).

He then proceeded to telephone Tina with his story of needing to find some young people for his mother, and said that he regretted that their evening had been so short – that before he left town perhaps she would have dinner with him. Tina was not fooled. Damn the man, she said to herself, and called Buddy.

“He’s coming over in two days,” she said, “How do we play this?”

Buddy said, “I’ll be there.”

So when Maximilian strolled over from his hotel to hers on one of the first days of July, he had polished his story – all he wanted was their address or phone number.

That was all, and then he would call his mother and have her come up and get introduced by someone. He wasn’t going to let this meeting become involved with gossip, rumour or people such as the Krazniks.

But he was impatient, and he didn't know about the steps taken by the First Secretary at his embassy to have him watched, nor could he suspect the presence of Buddy Holzer in the lobby of the George V with his camera. Maximilian phoned Tina from downstairs, but she asked him to come on up to room 202. It was because of this that Buddy was able to snap a picture of the two of them coming out of her room together.

Not only did Buddy's flash catch shock and anger on the face of His Excellency, Prince Maximilian, but another of his snatching for the camera. Half an hour later the discreet friend of the First Secretary, who had been reading a newspaper in the lobby and who happened to have joined Maximilian unobtrusively in the elevator, was having a very interesting business talk with Buddy Holzer in the hotel bar. Buddy, whose jaw Maximilian had just managed to reach, was being made aware that it would perhaps be easier and more profitable than he had had any idea of to help Tina out of her financial situation, and the swipe at the jaw needed to be avenged.

And Maximilian did not take Tina out to dinner that evening. He stayed behind only long enough to tell Tina what he thought of her in language obviously learned in the service to his Britannic Majesty, his uncle, in England, but he was sorry to have been unable to knock Buddy down, smash his face in, and the camera, too. Nothing could be worse than this.

He went back to his hotel in a sweat of anger. But also a feeling very like fear.

Perhaps the photographer was put onto Tina by her husband, he thought; on the other hand, the way she didn't look that surprised made him suspect blackmail, but whoever was responsible he knew the consequences of such a thing, and of such a picture, and at such a time! He hardly had the right to pursue a young girl of good family, he thought – not with the possibility of scandalous newspaper articles hanging over his head – and he still did not know where she was. Only the strongest feeling made him think it was more than a daydream brought on by incipient middle age – something any sensible person would tell him to forget all about.

It was ironic that all that his mother most dreaded should have come about just now – when he wanted to put all that behind him. There was irony in the justice of it all.

He could do no more about it until he had survived, or somehow avoided, a very nasty thing that might do infinite harm to his brother, as well as dash his nascent ideas of a better life.

Buddy and Tina lunched next day at the Tour d'Ivoire. They talked happily about plans. The pictures which Buddy had developed that night were terrific – made to order. They suggested guilt and even a little violence as Maximilian had reached for the camera. He could do something with these.

Chapter 8

The I Love Paris Ball began to be a subject of conversation at certain gatherings. John Trent and Pauly, flitting from auction to restaurant, and from restaurant to small dinner party, were approached by friends to escort some American women to the ball – women whose husbands, contacts of Bilco Oil, were in the United States.

They agreed to this although they later said to friends, "My dear, I mean really. Can you imagine actually calling anything the I Love Paris Ball? I mean, in cold blood? I said to Pauly, I really did, how much more tacky can you get?"

At the same time Henriette, the younger duchess, who had decided to direct Charlotte Schlemmer's efforts, took note of the fact that one of the de la Rocque girls was to represent both France and America. She said to her brother-in-law that although she hadn't met the girls or their mother, she understood they were charming, and she told Gérard that perhaps he should consider the older one as a bride himself: "You owe it to yourself to think of marriage," said Henriette.

Mrs. Schlemmer and the duke convinced several of the biggest American companies in Paris to join in the I Love Paris celebration of Franco-American relations, and doing something for the Historic Monuments at the same time. They were convinced to help the promotion and take a table of ten, and if they could not do so, to buy large ads in the Ball Programme. Mr. Ben Fazy not only had donated his Hôtel for the use of the ball, for which he hoped he would be remembered kindly by these members of French society, but also by the Society for the Preservation Historic Monuments, which he calculated might well include his own in their underwriting.

The older duchess had gone through the *Bottin Mondain*, compiling an invitation list; someone at the American embassy took care of the important Americans known to be in Paris – people who weren't attached to Bilco Oil.

There were seven American girls whose families had decided to take part in the ball, in addition to Patty Schlatz. They would all fly over together with their parents, three from Shaker Heights, two from Dallas; only two came from New York, and one of whom was the daughter of a director of Bilco.

Each family would come in with $5000, which seems like nothing now, but which at that time was a great deal of money, certainly $50,000 if it were to be done today. Airlines had been offered free tickets for a full color page in the programme. The girls were to be taken on a tour, and were promised to meet European high society.

A problem remained, however, as both Charlotte Schlemmer and Henriette de Ruissy knew, and that was getting some young men along. The cadets from St. Cyr and Polytechnique would help and would look fantastic; they would give the affair an official stamp, but most young men were now out of town and slippery at best.

The older duchess gave herself the task of a telephone campaign to anyone she knew who had a son the right age. She went personally to speak with the editors of the several newspapers that had Sunday special features on fashion and social events. Invitations were sent to editors of weekly magazines, to the European offices of the American press; further, the Duchess suggested to the editors that this was to be a tribute to a new era of international society, besides a tribute to the enduring memory of Lafayette, de Grasse, the Expedition of 1918, and the Normandy beaches.

The press was for the most part co-operative and agreed to run a story at the end of the week, a story that would name the girls, and mention the Preservation of Ancient Monuments; even editors of the leading liberal press were not above being co-operative with a Duchess in their offices, even to being invited to a table of special guests. A little later some of the far leftist papers said some rough things about capitalists and anachronistic class pressure, which they somehow worked into a number of diatribes on war-mongers, colonialism and Asian affairs.

On the first of July the seven girls, with at least one parent each, arrived in Paris accompanied by five photographers, and now Mrs. Schlemmer's real work began. Final plans for their hospitality were made. The people from her husband's office who were to organize the tours of Paris had to be checked with; the girls were to be taken to the Louvre, Notre Dame, for a bus ride through Paris, to the Flea Market and lunch in Montmartre. The presses that do the Bilco Oil stockholders reports printed up eight golden booklets with their schedule, with menus of what they ate, with cellophane windows for photographs and pages with blanks for names and addresses of people they met. These came with little golden pencils attached with gold thread.

The New York Times ran pictures of the girls and a story together with some candid shots taken by the photographers who accompanied them.

Our own photographer, who had been with me at the Ritz and had taken the photograph of Beatrice de la Rocque, also met them at the airport, as did I, in order for my *Where Are they now*? column to feature as a scoop.

All was going to plan.

****

For three days following his mother's drinks gathering Ivan sat in the cafés of the Left Bank in a very ugly mood. Paris was pretty dull, after all, and the Left Bank was phony. He didn't want to be trapped into becoming an escort for his mother.

Then he disappeared. The word went round among the people who knew him that he had suddenly left for London with Olivia Bryce-Smith, who had to go home to do a couple of shows. The Left Bank intellectuals were impressed with someone who could discuss Sartre one day, pick up models, and have the cash to fly to London on the spur of the moment.

Clarky got up the courage to invite Beatrice to the movies one evening; he mentioned that Ivan and Olivia and gone to London. He told her so that she wouldn't think that he had been interested in Olivia himself, although there was wistfulness in his voice because it seemed to him that Ivan could always whisk a girl off from under his nose – not that he had made an effort in that direction.

Beatrice, of course, didn't care one way or the other, which he could also tell. She thought they were all amazingly immature.

That evening Alex Feldenstein poured out a drink from his father's crystal decanter, a thing he did only when his father was out of town. He raised an eyebrow at Clarky, who had invited himself over. This eyebrow-lifting was a gesture he copied from his uncle and was meant to ask Clarky if he took soda.

"Seen anyone interesting?"

Clarkson glanced down at his recently buffed fingernails. He really hadn't done very much during the week other than going to the movie. He had changed hotels one day, having found one five francs cheaper and a little nearer his garage than the one he was in. He had had a haircut and manicure at the Ritz. He really hadn't seen anyone much, and it was why he had looked up Alex.

They were sitting in the private apartments of the Feldenstein's gallery. Two Titians and a Van Gogh looked down at them in this room which was furnished with reproduction Louis XVI chairs and an Aubusson carpet. The room looked out over the cobbled courtyard and high wrought iron gates that separated them from the rue du Faubourg St. Honoré.

"Nobody special, I guess."

Alex sat down on one of his mother's reproduction settees and crossed his legs the way his uncle did, and tweaked the crease along his trousers.

"You saw Tina at Ivan's. Didn't she look great?"

"She had some heavy date. Left early."

"Yeah? Anyone we know?"

"She didn't say who. I guess she was talking to the de la Rocque girls about their place."

"Is that right? I put her on to that. How are Beatrice and Francesca?"

"Fine, I guess. Beatrice is getting ready to come out at this deb ball."

“Which deb ball is that?”

“You remember. She was having her picture taken when we saw them in the Ritz.”

Alex sipped his drink and smoothed his hair.

“Right. The I Love Paris Ball, or some such thing. No kidding. She is? Isn’t that just a deal to soak Americans?”

“I guess not. Who’s the Duchesse de Ruissy?”

“Premier duchess, or some such thing. That fellow with Charlotte Schlemmer the other night is the Duke’s brother. She’s the head of the ball.”

“No kidding. I didn’t notice. I got an invite come to think of it, but I threw it in the basket.” Then after a moment, “Tell you what. I’ll go if you go.”

“I’m not invited.”

“Don’t be ridiculous, you know Beatrice.”

“Where’s Nevsky?”

“He’s in London, I guess.”

“What’s going on in London?”

“Dunno. He just went over for a coupl’a days, I guess. He went over with Olivia.”

Clarky smiled a rather sad smile when he said that.

“What? Bryce-Smith? You’re not serious.”

“I guess so.”

“Well, he can keep her for my money. Of course a guy like Nevsky can pick up anything. He just has to flash that Prince title around.”

“He doesn’t use that much.”

“Yeah, Clarky, but it’s there; Russian too. As a matter of fact we’re thinking of activating the title of Baron in our family. Boy would that help.”

“Are you a Baron?”

“Well, no, not exactly. But a lot of people call themselves Baron. We want to use it mostly in New York. Its uncle’s idea. He figures it would help the art business and I sure could use it.”

Alex tossed off the last of his brandy and soda and held his swizzle stick between his finger and thumb, pointing it at Clarky.

"Tell you what. I could use a trip to London right now. Why don't you and me go on over?"

"OK by me."

"We'll take Dad's plane. He's in Milan; won't be back till next week. He won't need it. I'll give the pilot a call."

Alex stood beside the boulle desk waiting while the gallery secretary put him through to the pilot, and Clarky stared up at the yellow satin curtains.

****

Through Olivia, whose number Clarky had, the two met up with Nevsky at the Mother's Love, off London's Sloane St., the latest watering hole for the young set. The Mother's Love had the strongest drinks and the loudest music in London, where the mod style had just been born and spread from Liverpool. Music, amplifiers and complex percussion were the flavour of the moment and at that time they were a novelty.

Ivan was found with Henry Alastair and Hugo Davenant, involuntarily down from Oxford for the rest of the term. Clarky said, "Hi There" and pulled up a small upside-down keg, which is what one sat on at the Mother's Love.

"What's up here?"

"My dear fellow, without wheels nothing's bloody well up."

Harry Alastair looked out from dark wavy hair – the envy of his friends. He wore his hair in a slightly tousled style. He was wearing a velvet jacket and a black string tie. He looked fed up.

He had two more weeks before the suspension of his driver's license was lifted. He was known to have a fierce grandfather in the House of Lords, who was not amused by his shenanigans.

"Nothing's going on anyway," said Hugo Davenant, in a spirit of comfort.

Ivan, waiting for Olivia to return from powdering her nose, was both bored and amused to think of Alex and Clarky having so little imagination as to follow him to London.

"What brings you over, Clarky? Nothing going on in Paris?"

"Sure," Clarky thought of something to say," but not till next week."

"What's going on then?"

"The I Love Paris Ball."

"What?"

Harry Alastair looked up again, "I say old man, you know, you really can't go to a party with a name like that. I mean, this I Love Paris thing. It sounds pretty unhealthy. What is it anyway?" (At that time Englishman still said, "I say," a catchphrase that has since subsided into the past.)

"Deb dance."

"My God! A deb dance! You're a big boy now. What in the name do you want to go to a deb dance for?"

"Girl I know's coming out, I guess. Alex is going."

Alex smoothed his hair. Harry Alastair had a way of making everything seem "out." Alex thought it was unfair – with Alastair's social position, he could afford to avoid everything. He explained a bit resentfully:

"This happens to be a charity ball run by the Duchesse de Ruissy. It should be worth looking into."

Ivan chimed in, "It's that girl we met at the Ritz, right? Isn't it some kind of promotion?"

To which Alex said, "It's for *Les Monuments Historiques*. They have taken over the *Hôtel Plessis* that that Egyptian is restoring. The champagne should be good."

Alex liked saying French words in a very French accent around his Anglo-Saxon friends.

Hugo Davenant was the quiet, fair-haired type of Englishman whose elders did not suspect of being a troublemaker because his hair was fair and not unreasonably long.

He said, “Might be a good thing to ensure it’s a good party – I mean, if you know someone who’s coming out, it would hardly be fair to let her be taken in by a lot of Americans and Egyptians.”

“How do you mean?”

Hugo, whose temporary absence from Magdalen College was due to his putting small mousetraps into the toes of the dean’s slippers, gazed at his friends innocently:

“I don’t know what you fellows think, but frankly, I resent people who give bad parties. Went to a bad party last month and haven’t got over it yet. It’s just an idea, of course, but if this girl is a friend of yours, I think we owe it to her to guarantee it’s a good party.”

“How’s that?”

“Up at Magdalen we have a first rate band, all friends of mine from Eton – we’re planning on performing at the Edinburgh Fringe next month. We could take ’em along, just in case we don’t care for the music at this party.”

Harry Alastair called for another Mother’s Milk, which at the Mother’s Love is almost straight gin.

“I have my pilot’s license. They haven’t suspended that; I can take some people over. Damn good idea. In fact, should have thought of it myself.”

When spoken to by Hugo, the leader of the band, Robert Robertson, a classics scholar, who had created and named the Homer’s Hummers band and written most of its songs, saw no problem in taking his group to Paris for a few days. They could try their new songs out before they took them to the Fringe.

Having crashed parties before, however, he warned Alastair and Davenant that he would have to be given the names of the people running the show in order to get in – in case there was any difficulty at the door. Carrying their band instruments might not be enough if they were also wearing their band uniform, which was a sheet worn in toga style and a wreath of laurel leaves.

Harry Alastair and Hugo Davenant didn’t know Ivan particularly well. Alastair had met him in New York when his father had been chairman of a mission to the UN. Hugo had seen him at Alastair’s party in London the summer before, and they weren't sure he was their sort, but as Harry said to Hugo, being rusticated without wheels was pretty dull – and it might help pass the time. He added that since Clarky was an American maybe they could get him to rent a car to take them all down to Newmarket to take in a couple of races.

This was not a success. Poorer than when they started, they were stopped on their way back to London for hopeless driving. Hugo, who happened to be at the wheel, pretended to be a deaf mute, Henry explained to the policeman that they were taking him back to the asylum, but that it was necessary that he drive, being the only who knew the way and had not been drinking. The policeman, who had a son of his own, smiled and limited himself to giving them a warning. It was beautiful weather and Olivia Bryce-Smith sat on the top of the back seat and waved at buses.

That was London in the sixties.

In Paris, sunlight shone on the *quais* along the Seine and the chestnuts were in full leaf. Even French people stopped for lunch on at the street-side restaurants and drank rosé under striped awnings.

The de la Rocques, mother and daughters, looked forward to the arrival of Xavier, husband and father. His seminar at the college finished, he would arrive in time for the ball – for him it would be an occasion to catch up with old friends.

That week Beatrice attended pre-ball dinners, but she was not included in the bus tour. The dinners were pleasant, she said, but the young men found to partner them were very young. She still thought about the man she had seen in the Ritz. The fact that she didn't know who he was, or have any practical idea of ever seeing him again, didn't make her sad – just a little pre-occupied.

She felt that the Universe took care of things, and that man had looked at her in a way that was almost frightening. On the one hand she felt it was quite disturbing and she would almost feel more like avoiding him than anything else, but on the other, if she ever saw him again he would deal with it, with her, with everything.

So she found the young men rustled up by the hostesses very young, and she became absent-minded.

She didn't want to disappoint the people who had made this event possible for her, but she did feel it was all about nothing much. The dress they had found at Castamagni was a true designer dress – simple, but immensely flattering, enhancing her tall figure. It had needed something done to the hem where a model had stepped on it, but no one would ever know.

While she was not part of the tour of Paris, she was included with the other girls when they were taken to the Hôtel Plessis for a rehearsal of the presentation two days prior to the ball.

The eight young girls and their fathers – or in the absence of fathers, their Parisian hosts – practiced their entrance and formal presentation. This included their pause at the top of the great staircase and the slow walk down it. At the bottom of the stairs, where they would face the ball's patrons, they practiced their deep curtsy, today to gramophone; on the day it would be to an orchestra.

It was planned by Mrs. Schlemmer that after this the girls and their parents would move down the line, being personally greeted by the guests of honour and joining it at the far end. They would thus add to the line, in order to greet the guests who would have gathered in the vestibule. Once all the girls, now joined by their mothers, had joined the line, the guests waiting in the vestibule would come down the line in their turn; they would then pass on through the honour guard of St. Cyr cadets, into the ballroom set up with round dinner tables – each seating eight or ten.

The last of the debutantes to come down the stairs was to be Beatrice, squired by her father and, arriving last, would stand beside the duchess in position to be the first to greet the guests as they went down the receiving line. This had been decided by Charlotte and Henriette, as she represented France.

The Hôtel was very hot that morning. There was an army of people cleaning, lighting was being wired, curtains were being hung either side of the great French windows that opened onto a broad terrace. Men were laying the red carpet that would soften the staircase; the chandelier was being washed in ammonia and warm water. Henriette de Ruissy and Charlotte Schlemmer directed it all while the debs practiced their curtsy and giggled together. Beatrice tried to be friendly with them, her sister helped the florist choose vases that were to be filled.

****

At the Prince de Galles hotel, meanwhile, Maximilian looked anxiously through the newspapers over a late breakfast. He had put a call in to Portugal to his mother. She would have to come to Paris to help him if and when the scandal broke, as it certainly would when the pictures were seen. She would stand by him and help him deny whatever he could. What a forlorn hope! Of course someone would publish or blackmail with those pictures, so hard to explain or deny.

He was in the process of running his eye down the social pages of the papers dreading what he might see, when he caught the name Beatrice de la Rocque Tourbonnière, under a small article mentioning the I Love Paris Ball. Here she was, to be presented with Americans. (Perhaps, he thought, they had gone to America after all.) The Duchesse Ruissy was an organizer – Well, that's not a problem! Maximilian had met Henriette. "Why, that old bat!" he said to himself, "I can get invited to that!"

And so he did.

Henriette was delighted to hear from him. "Can I come to your party?" he asked with the charm he used on hostesses.

"*Mais c'est formidable, c'est incroyable*" (But that's terrific, that's incredible!), she exclaimed. She told her mother-in-law the news from a pay-phone as there were as yet no telephones installed in the Hôtel Plessis.

Chapter 9

Mr. Ben Fazy had had the marble floors of the Hôtel Plessis scraped and polished, the parquet floors basically refinished and waxed in time for the ball and curtains hung.

During the past one hundred years, the Hôtel Plessis, situated in the old section of Paris known as *le Marais* (now a much visited tourist spot) had been progressively neglected, and in latter times squatted in by indigent Arab families; at the time of the I Love Paris Ball *le Marais* had not yet been cleaned up by André Maurois. Inches of wax and dirt had had to be scraped off the floors of the reception rooms, but fortunately for Mr Ben Fazy, having this done for the ball meant that these aspects of its restoration could be part of Bilco Oil's Public Relations expenses, and the budget for public relations at Bilco was large.

This would be welcome, even to someone as rich as Ben Fazy, who did not hesitate to point out that he was putting a large sum into this event. The curtains, for instance, were paid for by Ben Fazy himself, but the surcharge for having them done in a rush had to be paid for, to say nothing of the lighting.

Finally the day arrived.

On the big night the cars began to arrive – members of the reception committee, Mrs. Ben Fazy, the younger duchess, the Schlemmers, were all delighted with the look of everything. Golden chairs had been rather awkwardly placed in the marble hall at the bottom of the stairs down which the debs were to appear. These were for the special guests who had agreed to attend the ball at the request of the duchesses.

These honorees were the wives of the men who were on the duke's board of the Society for the Preservation of Historic Monuments and included some distinguished names. There were also the wives of several government ministers or their representatives – the Minister of the Interior and the Minister of Education, for instance.

The only people missing were young men. There were few of these, almost none, other than the cadet honour guards. But the vestibule began to fill up.

The debs had been there since much earlier. They were upstairs in one of the few rooms that had been furnished and restored. The girls still felt a bit awkward with their new hairdos, and peered over each other's shoulders into the big gold framed mirror.

"I guess the French don't know about air conditioning," said a deb from Dallas, whose father was a director of Bilco. But hot as it was the girls noticed that there was a patch of cold in the room – a cold patch which Mr. Ben Fazy tried vainly to understand. Finally, he had convinced himself it was some kind of draught. Actually, it was a chilled spot, the centre of the haunting of the building – an odd chill that had made it so unpleasant for the many indigent Arab families who had squatted there in the recent past.

In 1747, François, Marquis de Montforais, strangled his wife in this place, and himself was stabbed to death by his valet, her lover. The valet was duly arrested and executed. There may have been extenuating circumstances which history does not record, however, for it is the Marquis that haunts the house and not the valet. There is, in the collection of Mr. and Mrs. Louis B. Stranahan of New York, a portrait of the Marquise de Montforais in a riding habit and three-cornered hat, with a young man standing nearby holding her horse. I like to think that this was the young man who killed the husband – an unpleasant man by all accounts.

This night, however, the night of the I Love Paris Ball, the unpleasant ghostly presence of the Marquis made no impression on the activities, which were far too crowded and too loud for it to make itself felt.

Beatrice had dressed at home and had arrived with her parents and sister to join the girls upstairs. Her mother and sister had dressed her hair up behind a small diamond bracelet that looked like a miniature tiara. The girls she found upstairs were all afraid that they might perspire in the heat and ruin their dresses and clog the lacquer in their hair. Francesca tried to open a window, but Beatrice said, "On don't bother, Fran, it just doesn't matter."

She still seemed to be somewhat detached from it all. None of it seemed what she considered adult: either it was just New York all over again, or a bit childish. Her parents and sister were waiting with the other anxious parents in the vestibule when they were approached by the duke, handsomer than ever in white tie and tails. In his hand he had notes for the opening remarks he was to make.

With Mrs. Schlemmer he had decided not to mention Bilco Oil, but to stick with Lafayette, De Grasse and the American Expeditionary Force of 1917, in honour of which they had hung the rooms with French and American flags. They thought it better not to mention a major American financial body – feelings in France were still too sensitive about what some considered the economic neo-colonialism of the United States, which was how many regarded the generosity of the Marshal Plan.

There was to be a slight change of plan, he said with his charming shake of the head: because, after all, they had only the one French debutante, he proposed that it should be he that presented Beatrice rather than her father. It would give a better impression of French participation as the host country.

From upstairs the girls could hear the orchestra and the growing buzz of voices. Mrs. Schlemmer had been able to get the services of a fashionable party orchestra called *Le Coeur de Paris*, but not until the cadets arrived could the ball be said to have begun. Small clots of very young men, sent by friends of the Dowager Duchess, began to arrive. They stood in little groups and smoked. Mr. Ben Fazy flinched as he saw ashes fall on his brand new floor. But he knew better than to try to stop young Frenchmen from smoking.

The cadets from the two academies, St. Cyr and the Polytechnique, had arrived. The St. Cyriens were to form an honour guard for the guests to pass through into the larger room set up with the tables for dinner. There was a roll of drums which announced the beginning of the presentations. The debs' fathers had been brought upstairs and shown where to line up for the descent down the scarlet carpeted stairs. The fathers were very nervous and several of the debs asked their fathers to take their glasses off. Beatrice waited with the duke.

Maximilian must have arrived a few minutes earlier. He was in white tie and tails with his red ribbon and star. He joined the Dowager Duchess, who stood beside him, and a quick message was sent up to alert the nervous girls upstairs: when they reached the floor they were to curtsy deeply toward the man next to the duchesse, who would be royalty – then they were to curtsy to the Dowager Duchess, and go down the line of sponsors shaking hands. When they reached the end of the line they were to join it with their father, and their mothers would come to join them there.

The girls all followed one another, then, finally, the barker announced,

"Representing France, Mlle. Beatrice de la Rocque Tourbonnière, presented by the Duc de Ruissy."

The orchestra broke into the *Marseillaise*. No one minded that this – the anthem of the Revolution – was as unsuited to the 18th century house, the Duc de Ruissy or the Historic Monuments, as it could be. They were used to it.

There was a distinct murmur as Beatrice and the duke descended the stairs. Cameras popped. Beatrice wore the charming but detached manner I had noticed in the Ritz weeks earlier; it gave her a regal manner. Whether, I wondered, this was actually her eyesight, or because she was singularly free of vanity, rare in such a good looking girl, was hard to say. This was a picture that would do well in our magazine.

When Beatrice reached the floor she curtsied toward the figure next to the duchess... it was the man from the Ritz.

Maximilian, who watched her come down the stairs on the duke's arm and curtsy – and she had curtsied to him first as the highest in rank – was stunned to see that she looked up at him with recognition.

Like the other girls, she took her place in the reception line; it seemed natural to her that she now stood between the duke and Maximilian. Her parents came and stood next to them and the duchesses.

The guests filed through, Beatrice shook hands automatically with the new arrivals; but as she did so, she felt that at last everything made sense. Cameras flashed; she did not notice them. She only noticed that the man beside her had a deep voice and that he was there – a grown up. The dancing began. It was for the duke to open the ball with Beatrice, but the duchesses told him he must offer his place to Maximilian.

For Maximilian, still struck by the way she had looked at him – as if they had met before – this should have been a supreme moment. Further, it was the ideal manner in which to make his first appearance with Beatrice, and to meet her parents under the aegis of the premier duke and duchess of France – with no gossip, nothing vulgar, no rumours. It should have been ideal to be seen dancing with her – opening a well publicized ball for charity. His mind raced – the announcement of their engagement should have been made in the same way through the proper channels, but none of this could happen now.

For Maximilian the situation was laced with anger and anxiety, and not a little irony. Here she was at his side, the girl he had decided would make sense of the next phase of his life – beautiful and still – someone he felt he had known all his life. There were her parents, pleasant distinguished people, but he now faced a problem for which he had no answer.

That very morning he had received a call from his brother's secretary in Peltz. They had been contacted by an anonymous individual who had photographs to sell – compromising photographs, which, so they were informed, would bring scandal to the royal family, just as they were facing Parliamentary elections.

Maximilian had to listen while he was told, tactfully of course, that this was not an expense his brother should be asked to pay out of his budget, nor would the government do it, and the possible scandal could affect the future of his country; paying might be the only answer.

On Maximilian asking how the situation was left they said they were playing for time – stalling. They had not asked the amount they were asking; they had taken a contemptuous line, saying that they had threatening calls of this type every day and would have to have proof that the pictures actually existed. But of course, even if they agreed to pay their demands, there was no guarantee that copies would not continue to be a threat or to circulate.

And Maximilian did not yet know that the situation was actually worse than this. The First Secretary at the embassy had indicated to Buddy Holzer that if nothing came across as money from the prince or his family, he knew people in the anti-monarchy party that would be happy to buy them.

He did his best to seem normal, circled the floor with Beatrice and sat with her parents. He engaged her father in a conversation about international finance, while at the back of his mind he was trying to find a way to suggest that the family visit Kravonia before going back to the United States. They could stay at the residence in Peltz – his mother would come up from Cascais.

But nothing could be said or done now with imminent blackmail demands and scandal about to hit the press: those damning pictures would certainly give the appearance of his being the worst kind of womanizer, frequenting third rate people. There might be a publicized divorce, detective's evidence.

They would have to be bought. How much? What surety? And as the official in Peltz had pointed out, what guarantee could be had that all the pictures were sent to him or destroyed.

He had not listened to his mother; he had not done his duty; he had not taken account of the kind of people he was seen with; now he may have ruined his life just as he knew what it should be. And perhaps he had done irresponsible damage to his brother and the political climate of his country. He actually felt a cold sweat.

There was something else: the girl had looked at him with what looked like recognition; and now her manner seemed so natural, almost trusting. What would she think when she saw pictures of him, coming out of Tina's room, attacking a photographer. Not one of the dangerous sports in which he had engaged during his long bachelorhood had given him this cold sense of fear.

The duke, charming as ever, made his brief remarks about Lafayette and the Normandy Beaches; dinner was served. The Schlemmers and the Schlatzes congratulated themselves on a huge success. The ball was going well. Mr. Schlatz pointed out how right he was that it was quite possible to assemble High Society if you put your mind to it – even royalty. Everything was going according to plan: the cadets did their duty by the American girls, although the young men rounded up by the hostesses had a tendency to stand around.

Later, when dessert had been dealt with, Maximilian, Xavier de la Rocque and Beatrice moved into the small adjoining salon where it was easier to talk.

As the dancers circled, Francesca was sitting at the floor side table assigned to her parents when a voice beside her said, "You must let me sit here, they have taken my chair." It was Olivier de Ruissy, looking lanky and relaxed and a little bit untidy. "It is your sister, I think, with the prince."

He went on, "I am here with my grandmother, but she does not dance, and I am hiding from the American debutantes. You must protect me."

They spoke on; she thought him nice. He thought her different; it was rare he met a girl who understood both the French and American cultures.

****

That was what was going on inside the building; outside something else was happening. Outside, Homer's Hummers had arrived carrying their instruments, and more to the point, their amplifiers.

Wearing their signature togas and laurel leaves, they brought everything into the marble hall adjoining the ball room, where the tables had been prepared and served with dinner from the Tour d'Ivoire. The Hummers set up their instruments next to the door, and having found the electrical outlets, plugged in adaptors, and hit the big beat.

Robert Robertson, his laurel leaves a little askew with the effort of helping his drummer set up the percussion section, electrified everyone within earshot with "*I'll Make Any Bird Sing*" – a great success later that year at the Edinburgh Fringe, and which sold thousands in recording.

Harry Alastair began to dance, slender and graceful with long fine hands that gave elegance to every extraordinary movememt. Hugo Davenant, smaller and slighter, was also capable of unique gyrations. Robert Robertson's amplifiers were the latest and loudest. The sound of his boast about making any bird sing throbbed through the Hôtel Plessis with a depth of torrid sound that even the dowagers responded to unconsciously before they realized that it was the most dreadful of all cultural imports from *les Îles Britanniques* – what the French called *le Yeh Yeh.*

Within the space of a song, the eight American debs had heard the new English sound, born in Liverpool and imitated by many, and they had responded with a rush to the central hall and kicked off their shoes. The fact that no young Frenchmen followed them and that cadets from two academies watched in fascination didn't stop them, either. The new style of music and dance had not yet descended on Paris, and with those dances you don't need partners – besides, Alastair could partner any number of girls.

Clarky, Alex and Ivan – who had brought along Olivia Bryce-Smith in entirely the wrong dress – sat at the spare table that had been assigned to them at the back of the dining room. They were not sure how to react; they had never believed that Homer's Hummers would actually turn up. Now that they had, they rather envied their English friends their enterprise in actually pulling a thing like this off and not just talking about it – but something told them that they were in for trouble.

As they saw the younger duchess of Ruissy move into action, the three of them tried to look disassociated from it all and, discretion being the better part of valour, they signaled silently to each other by eye-rollings that an exit should be found.

Henriette de Ruissy made the mistake of thinking that young people have a latent spirit of obedience that can be aroused if one sounds definite enough. They don't, and the duchess sounding definite did not rise above Homer's Hummer's version of "*Baby, You Can Mend My Car*," which Robertson accented with electronically produced sounds of car squealings, crashes and hootings.

Henriette got hold of Mrs. Schlemmer, who with Mr. Ben Fazy, got the head caterer. No one really seemed to be in charge. The older women and Frenchmen commented that it was very odd of the organizers to have engaged such a modern alternative band. They whispered to each other that it was the American influence and that it was inevitable that a decline in manners and morals would accompany any bridging of the gap between Old France and the Moderns.

Charlotte Schlemmer saw sooner than did the duchess that the head caterer could not handle the situation and told him that if he expected any remuneration for his services, he would see to it that his waiters threw the Hummers out. The Hummers were barefoot and their hairy English legs appeared below their draped togas. The head caterer, who had done business with American firms before, knew how difficult collection could be and how complicated getting them to a French claims court. He brought out some of the younger waiters to the attack. It was definitely what could be called a mistake.

Someone, in an attempt to unplug the Hummer's amplifiers and electrical instruments, unplugged the wrong cord and plunged much of the downstairs, still in the process of being re-wired by Ben Fazy's team, into darkness.

There were screams. An American deb let out a long, hysterical scream – a scream that had been building up in her since her arrival in Paris and the endless formality of the week's doings. It was also her first opportunity to have an unlimited supply of Piper Heidsieck. There was something communicative in her scream. Perhaps she was the one from Dallas – there was a touch of infinity in the wild freedom of her screaming that would have brought little dogies all the way from Wyoming at a trot.

At any rate, the excitement even got to some of the Frenchmen, normally bound in by mathematics exams and preparations for the *bac* and various *Écoles Supérieures*. In the darkness the crowd broke into two factions: those for and those against.

Waiters and the contemporaries of the duchess were on one side, backed by cadets encumbered with dress swords and epaulettes, versus American debs and those of the young French boys, found by the

Dowager Duchess, who took advantage of the darkness to express themselves – some for the first time.

There was something about Robert Robertson's "*Don't, don't leave me now*" that somehow helped. Now that the lower floor of the Hôtel was in darkness, there was no way of silencing their instruments and two of the guitarists had climbed up onto the stone balustrade that ran around the terrace outside the lower rooms. The great French windows, which opened onto this terrace, were crowded with people leaving the ballroom. Now the deb from Dallas was up there too – she had seized on the idea that Paris was more than history and these boys spoke English!

Meanwhile, Maximilian, Beatrice and her father were in the smaller salon where there was still light. They were unaware of the chaos in the front hall. Maximilian was looking remarkably like the portrait of his father which hangs in the Fisheries Guild Dining Hall in Peltz – without the beard, of course. He was thinking desperately. He needed to find a way to stay in touch with Beatrice's father – at the same time thinking through many plans for dealing with the scandal he expected to break in the next few days – unless he could deal with the blackmailers.

As chaos began to accelerate in the dining room, the girl's mother, Catherine, quietly joined her husband, daughter and Maximilian in the smaller salon.

Now in the ballroom someone had called the police – it was mostly likely Sidney Schlatz, who had gone outside; he had probably insisted that Ben Fazy put the call through.

Police vehicles were arriving at that moment with the familiar *pin pon pin pon* sound of the Parisian sirens. In the tall windows leading to the balcony there was the silhouette of Harry Alastair leading the dance. The ghost of the duc de Monplaisant was certainly not noticeable that evening.

My cameraman was happy for the first time as he dodged around to catch his shots. The photographers from the Paris press, who did not like this kind of assignment, had spent part of the evening with half a cigarette hanging out of the corners of their mouths, cameras in one hand, talking about wide lenses with a couple of the photographers who had come over with the debs.

One of them had been a war correspondent at one time and his hobby was sports photography; an evening spent like this annoyed him. He had got a couple of good shots of Maximilian in the style his magazine liked, but the screams of the girl from Dallas had suddenly brought him into action. There were silhouettes of guitarists against the roofs of Le Marais that made his evening worthwhile.

Having an eye for action he, too, climbed on to the terrace balustrade with his back supported by the building just as the police van arrived with officers within, as well as riding on the running boards. The sight of police always has an unfortunate affect on young people. Someone threw a wine glass at someone, and even some of the French wives with names like de la Connotière, du Frezac and de Monburzon threw themselves into the fray; it was hard to tell whose side they were on.

Six people quietly slipped outside into the innocent darkness of the street. Two of these were Olivier de Ruissy, who tapped Francesca on the shoulder and said that it was his opinion that "Less is more," and quietly guided her outside. He added, "*Ça va tourner mal*" (This is going to end badly). The others, Clarky, Alex and Ivan, with Olivia Bryce-Smith in tow, did likewise; they stood in the shadows and said very little, wondering if any of this would be linked to them.

At that moment Harry Alastair jumped off the balcony onto the roof of the police van, momentarily without a driver, and got behind the steering wheel. When the fire truck, which also arrived, gestured for it to make room, he backed it into the street.

There were more shouts, but the fire truck maneuvered into the courtyard. That was all he actually did, but the legend grew that he had driven away into downtown Paris with the police van, a story he still denies to this day, although the story is very tenacious and still told by everyone.

Personal feelings will get involved in occasions like this and a St. Cyrien cadet officer accidentally made an unfortunate remark to a Polytechnien cadet as he pushed past him. This was enough to cause an attack on the men of St. Cyr by the group of dark uniformed, cock-hatted Polytechniciens. Between the two groups of young rival Frenchmen the police moved in.

Two other police vans arrived on the scene at this moment but were blocked by the arrival of the delivery vans bringing the late supper from the Tour d'Ivoire. An altercation started between the chef and the police officers. Trays of edibles jostled by the crowd were strewn across the pavement as they were carried toward the building, five hundred miniature strawberry tarts, five hundred eclairs and five hundred.... It was a mess.

The crowd, which had now gathered outside the gates of the Hôtel, did not know what it was all about, but they yelled "*Algérie française*" and "*À la lanterne les capitalistes*" anyway. Someone yelled "*Ça ira.*"

The ball was over.

No one noticed Sidney Schlatz's wife, who was still sitting at their table more or less paralyzed by the confusion around her. Patty sat nearby having kicked off her shoes and told her mother she had never wanted to come to France. Taxis took disheveled girls and their angry mothers homeward to their hotels.

I thought, a bit ruefully, that the "*Where are they now?*" column would have to be carefully written.

At some point during all this, Homer's Hummers had simply disappeared. No one saw them go. Only one electrical cord was left to show they had been there.

It was over. Everything was over.

In the courtyard people stepped carefully over the miniature éclairs and *tartes au fraise* all over the ground. There was no late supper at the Hôtel Plessis that night. Someone, again probably Mr. Ben Fazy himself, plugged the lights back on.

****

Actually, no harm had in fact been done. The big room with the dining tables looked untidy – there were a few broken glasses and the tablecloths were disarranged. The orchestra, *Le Coeur de Paris,* came back from the kitchen area looking sheepish. Almost all the guests had gone outside.

The police saw no one to arrest.

Charlotte Schlemmer found her husband and the duke sitting on the scarlet carpet of the stairs of honour sick with laughter, wiping their eyes. They had never liked the idea of the ball in the first place. She was indignant.

Sidney Schlatz said he was going to sue. It wasn't at all clear who he meant to sue or how. It was just his natural reaction. No one paid much attention.

The three most responsible for the disaster – Clarky, Alex and Ivan – slipped away unnoticed. Clarkson was a bit sad – he had actually enjoyed meeting the duchess as he went down the reception line and had noticed Beatrice standing next to the prince. Clarky had a secret crush on Beatrice which would last him many years.

Although he would never have found the nerve to court Beatrice, and would not have had the nerve to ask her to dance, he nevertheless felt a little proud of having been beaten to the draw by a prince. The fact that he loses all his girls to someone else is exemplified by this failure. He and Alex had spoken with the younger duchess before the Hummers broke out. They had stood beside her in the dining room and Alex had said he had had the pleasure of meeting her brother-in-law.

Gérard himself had enjoyed the first part of the evening. He had quite a bit of the Piper Heidseick and wore his Charles Boyer manner. He danced with the young girls and recognized Clarky and Alex.

"Ah, my young (he pronounced the "g" in young) American friend – you have met my sister-in-law," and acknowledging Alex, he said,

"This is M. Feldenstein the younger, who was telling me so interestingly of our charming debutante's family, and their plans to rent Tourbonnière to Hollywood," he winked at her.

"*Mais ça m'intéresse beaucoup*!" (But that interests me greatly) had said the duchess. She had mentioned the matter quite casually to Beatrice, but Beatrice seemed to know very little about it. She had only said that Mrs. Kraznik, or her husband, had said something about wanting to see it, but it was all in her father's hands.

The duchess had shot a meaningful glance at her brother-in-law. How men were stupid, she thought; he should have realized that it was through the Feldensteins that people such as the Krazniks would have to be reached. He should have told her sooner.

Gérard had then said to Clarky, "Perhaps you too will be in Normandy the summer?"

Clarky had responded, "I don't know. Maybe, I guess. The de la Rocques are going there in a couple of days."

"It is an old place," Gérard had continued, "not of great interest historically or architecturally, as you will see if you visit. It is of sentimental value to the region only."

"It cannot compare with Ruissy, of course," had interposed Henriette, "but there is only one Ruissy. Perhaps you will both be in Normandy to see your friends. You must stop past and see Ruissy. We are very fond of Americans." Alex and Clarky had looked at each other.

"Perhaps," she went on, "you will go with your Hollywood friends. It might interest them to see our Ruissy and it is not so far from Tourbonnière."

For Clarky, this was finally what he expected of France – the kind of thing he imagined being said at Parisian parties – duchesses suggesting that you and your art connoisseur friend drop by their castle any time you were in the neighborhood. He would have tried to firm it up into an invitation for the weekend if he could have thought how.

It was at that moment that Homer's Hummers had broken into song; the duchess had gasped with shock – she had been about to have gone to find Xavier de la Rocque in order to ask him particulars concerning location filming, but this invasion had to be dealt with.

For their part Clarky and Alex had felt almost as shocked as the duchess; they could see trouble coming and had moved surreptitiously to their table at the back of the room hoping that no one would connect them with Harry Alastair's idea of a joke.

There had been other familiar faces among the early arrivals before the trouble began: John Trent and Pauly had been invited to escort grass widows and balance out tables, as they frequently were. And while Clarky and Alex had been speaking with the duchess they had sipped champagne in the small drawing room off the ballroom; the room had been hung with yellow brocade curtains in time for the occasion, but only furnished with groups of chairs.

They couldn't make up their minds what they were going to say about the ball. On the one hand it was an obvious promotion and just a crude imitation of what took place in every socially conscious city in the United States; on the other hand, the duchess was the real thing – so was Maximilian of Hohen-Zeitfest. They also had recognized the girl he had been dancing with, and there they were chatting with her father. Maybe they were in on to something. The American boys were familiar and the French boys looked shy. The champagne was first class, but that might be just the power of Bilco Oil. Certainly, the almighty American dollar was encroaching everywhere.

They had decided it was a sign of the times that even a French ball raising money for the preservation of Historic Monuments, and presided over by a real duchess with royalty present, was dependent on the dollar.

And they had liked meeting the duchess. As a matter of fact, one of John Trent's most regular correspondents, who happened to be the society editor on one of the more important New York papers, mentioned in an article shortly afterwards that, "No hostess can be more gracious than the Duchesse de Ruissy recently seen in a dark russet silk gown trimmed with feathers, welcoming guests to her husband's fund-raiser, the I Love Paris Ball. The ball was held for the benefit of the Preservation of Historic Monuments and graced by a bevy of charming debutantes from the other side of the water."

It was notable that the article did not mention Sidney B. Schlatz nor their daughter, Patty, but did go on to say, "Among the distinguished guests were John Trent and Paul Sanders, in Paris for the summer." And, "It is a shame that in an age where graciousness is at a premium the bad manners of youth today drew an abrupt end to the kind of occasion rarely seen in this century."

By which one can see that in the end John and Pauly had decided to approve the event. They, too, thought perhaps a trip to Normandy could be in order.

However, there were other reports in the press. Several issues of London's Standard and other broadsheets ran stories – and expensively acquired photographs – about the event later that week. They captioned them: "The Hon. Harry Alastair, heir to the Avon title, leads the biggest gate-crashing incident in Parisian history" – and "American debs flee with the Hon. Hugh Davenant and Harry Alastair as police officers arrive."

Another read, "Classics scholars, led by Robert Robertson, steal police van." This was obviously a complete fabrication suggested by a photographer.

Maximilian with Beatrice and her parents had remained in the salon throughout what the French called the *brouhaha.* While Maximilian had made conversation about international finance, he was actually trying to get the de la Rocques to suggest that he come out to Normandy for a day while they were visiting their aunt. He had hinted that he might be going past Ruissy for a weekend.

****

That evening Tina Kraznik went to Orly to pick up Sam.

Next morning Maximilian put a call through to his brother's aide in Peltz to ask if they had heard anything more about the pictures. The answer was No, but the aide reminded Maximilian that they had told the negotiator they would want details, proof and clarity before they even considered the matter, or believed it was not a hoax. They had given the impression that they thought the whole matter a fraud. They had the understanding they would hear again with details and the amount they wanted in a matter of days. It was obvious that the aide in Peltz was trying to remain respectful, but Maximilian suspected that he had less respectful thoughts in reserve. This was an appalling thing to have happen to his brother.

However, the more time went by, the lesser the impact. This had to be good news. Nothing had happened yet. Maximilian had said he would call again every few days.

Chapter 10

When Xavier de La Rocque had ended his seminar and prepared to join his wife and daughters in Paris, he had thought it would merely be a pleasant way to see his attractive daughters enjoy themselves, and he could catch up with relatives he had not seen for a considerable time.

In those days going to Europe was not like today. In those days one took a ship. It was something of a production: getting the tickets, choosing the stateroom, allowing for five days at least from shore to shore, then the boat train to the capital. Today, with the instant flights and constant travel, one has forgotten not only the charm, but the hassle and the complications of international travel of the time.

Now, as he arrived in Paris, he found that there was something else: when he arrived his wife mentioned to him that some movie people had asked about his aunt's house in Normandy, and she had suggested they telephone when he arrived. He didn't think much about it – although perhaps there would be something of financial interest for his poor old aunt. And he put it out of his mind.

He was surprised a few days later when he did, in fact, get a call from someone calling himself Kraznik, as if he was supposed to know him. Mr. Kraznik did indeed say he was looking for an authentic location for a movie in France and had heard that his family owned a place with an old tower. The tower was important to the movie.

Xavier said he could see no objection to someone coming out and looking at the property. He would tell the lady of the house when he saw her in a few days. He realized that dollars paid in America might be a real advantage to his aunt and again did not think much more about it. He assumed an agent of some kind would get in touch to make an appointment to view the place. He might have phrased it differently had he been more familiar with Kraznik's methods and Hollywood in general.

****

Queen Helen received a telegram from her son (everything was done by telegraph in those days) which said, “Come to Paris immediately Maman - stop - Someone for you to meet - stop - I might need your help - stop - Max.” A little alarmed, she telephoned to have her apartments made ready – she would arrive in a week.

Each day Maximilian went through all the newspapers that had society and gossip news. Nothing yet.

Maximilian had decided that other than the possibility of having to negotiate with blackmailers, the best strategy would be to have his mother with him and possibly release photographs of himself at the ball, perhaps even pictures of his dancing with Beatrice, taken before it descended into chaos. It might be hopeless but at least the press should have a counter-image to present.

He thought it would be his best bet to drive out into Normandy, dropping by Tourbonnière. He would say he was on his way to Ruissy, where the ducal family had suggested he come for a weekend. What would they think of the pictures if he had not found a way to scotch the whole thing by that time? Other than paying, he could think of nothing.

His mother would arrive in a week.

But the First Secretary at the Embassy added to the personal file, in which he had Buddy Holzer’s telephone number. He forwarded these to the contacts he had in Kravonia, who sent word that they could buy the pictures if blackmail failed. The First Secretary agreed, but said that if they bought them he expected a commission.

He further added to the file clippings from the English press about Homer’s Hummers and Harry Alastair on the roof of the police van in case they came in useful somehow. He knew Maximilian was there.

The First Secretary had been delighted to hear that the Prince had been seen dancing with the American girl; who knew how much they couldn’t get out of the Kravonians for hushing up a big scandal at such a time? Queen Helen was coming to Paris in a week’s time. She would be the one to approach – he would need that photograph of Max and Mrs. Kraznik very soon.

In London, Harry's mother, Lady Alastair, arrived from the north, cutting short her tour of duty as lady-in-waiting, and scolded her son. If this went on, she said, his father and she would insist that he spend the summer vacation showing trippers around Alastair Court, which would be the end of his summer plans. She actually didn't mean this and hoped it wouldn't happen, as who knew what he and Hugo would do with their collection of antique cars – race them to Scotland and back in all likelihood.

Hugo Davenant's father, easily amused, and fond of his son, had straightened his face by the time he next saw Hugo and told him he wanted him to get a real summer job. Hugo did this, and, by dint of the fact he was reading anthropology at Oxford, was able to join a student team on an archaeological site in Lebanon. He would come back tanned, blonder than ever, having planted a fake fertility symbol among his team's finds.

Robert Robertson composed two more songs for the Edinburgh Fringe. One was called, "*A Night in Paris, Oh, Oh, Oh.*"

****

Sam Kraznik spent three days in Paris, a little surprised by and suspicious of the affectionate manner of his wife. He wanted to get back to London, he said, and his plans for *Breath of Drums*. Nevertheless, as he had agreed to do, he had put through the call to de la Rocque – it might work for the *By Kiss* project; he didn't mind taking a look at the location site she talked about.

Tina had an emergency meeting with Buddy Holzer, who had been told that further contact had been made with the people in Kravonia. His negotiator had insisted that the pictures be used within two weeks – before Maximilian left town and the pictures grew old. They discussed amounts and how they would divide the money.

Buddy agreed to follow the Krazniks into Normandy, both to offer Tina moral support and to get pictures that might be used to show Sam's mental cruelty toward her if it came to divorce, or she was charged with playing around. Tina told her husband that she had persuaded Buddy to come and take stills of the location, although she knew that was not necessary as Sam had his own team with him, as well as the scriptwriter who had done the adaptation of the novel.

In Paris, the duke and duchess barely spoke for the three days following the ball. Gérard and his brother smiled continually in a way that infuriated the younger duchess. That they could think such a thing funny! Why did they not pursue those Englishmen? Call the Embassy? It was disgraceful! It had been a wonderful idea, the ball, she said. They had made money for the society, but they could never do it again. She and Charlotte Schlemmer hardly knew how to speak of it, but it did cement their friendship. Henriette made Charlotte promise she and her husband would come to Ruissy in the forthcoming days and rest after all that horror.

They agreed that having Maximilian there had at least given the event elegance. She was also very gracious to the de la Rocques as the girl and Maximilian had really saved appearances in a way. She enjoyed speaking with Catherine de la Rocque, as it appeared that Prince Maximilian had paid them a formal call the day following the disaster. If anything came of that at least she could be recognized as being the instrument that brought the families together – there was always that. She suggested to them, also, that they come by Ruissy when in Normandy and wondered secretly if they would tell her who had suggested using their château as a film location.

She had to speak with the parents of the American debs, though – and none of the conversations were pleasant.

Now that he was in Paris, Xavier found it far more entertaining than he had expected. Like the duke, Gérard and Carl Schlemmer, he was more entertained than shocked by the chaos of the Bilco Ball, as it came to be known. He was a popular professor in part because he enjoyed the spirit and antics of undergraduates, and he was not at all surprised by the Homer's Hummers or the behavior of the guests.

Nor was he fooled by Maximilian's conversation about international finance; it was obvious to him that the Prince wanted to know Beatrice's father. His grey eyes narrowed with humour when he thought of it, because, after all, he was still a Frenchman.

Chapter 11

Somewhere between the towns of Lisieux and Nagère there is a small road that leads through long kilometers of forested and partly forested ground. Where this leads off the main route nationale there is a sign that says "Tourbonnière 15 km" with a picture of a little tower, which means you are coming to an historic château, a named tourist site.

That is now, but then there was no such sign and someone looking for the road would have to move slowly.

The village of Tourbonnière is a group of simple houses placed at convenient distances from each other, which removes the necessity of streets – a car can simply be driven around and about the houses. The whole overlooks a green, still river in which reeds grow; it has large stones on its banks on which household washing was done by village girls kneeling by the water's edge and beating it – in the sixties this was growing less frequent as more modern ways of doing laundry had begun to reach the depths of countryside.

As is often seen in that region of France, a tall crucifix and holy figures of a wayside *Calvaire* stands on the edge of the road; to this a jumble of telephone wires had been attached, awaiting the replacing of the main telephone pole that fell down in a record storm a year or two since.

In the village of Tourbonnière the residents will show you this *Calvaire* and tell you that this was where five aristocrats were killed during the Revolution, this event being fresher in their minds than the day when an English paratrooper came down in the tree above it during the Normandy landings. He had hung there helplessly until brave villagers brought him down and hid him from Germans still in the vicinity. Recent history lacks the lustre of tradition.

In the village of Tourbonnière there is a post office, though it did not stock air mail stamps, and a telephone central, which insures that there are no secrets in Tourbonnière. It was a square cement building with small windows decorated with a few geraniums, which did not do well in a northern climate.

There was a village parish school taught by two nuns – one was heavy and one was thin – Soeur Marie and Soeur Blanche; they were at daggers drawn with the village priest, and there was a state school which vied with them for attendance.

The sisters do not like the priest because he is from Le Mans and is a *sacré petit Breton* for one thing, and for another he brought some books on teaching New Math and wanted to use them in the school. As Soeur Blanche will explain to anyone, it is a great responsibility one takes to modernize the young; everyone knows that which is modern is dangerous.

The last priest in Tourbonnière gave courses in where babies came from with the result that several of the village girls became pregnant the following summer. As they explained to the old countess at the château, it was *Monsieur le curé* who had explained to them what it was all about; they had not understood it was wrong when he said that nature's way is God's way.

On feast days a procession was still made around the village with the priest surrounded by the school children dropping rose petals, and Soeur Blanche and Soeur Marie hustling the others along after them. This procession leads to the *Calvaire* and back to the village again.

The two sisters could be seen hitting little boys on the head when they sang "*Je suis crétin*" (I am an idiot) instead of "*Je suis Chrétien*" (I am a Christian) in the age-old tradition of French schoolboys. The sisters could be heard saying, "*Va t'en, va t'en*" to the two village curs that frisked along beside the procession, pulling the sashes of the little girls and barking merrily.

In the spring and summer the sisters used to keep a wary eye on the entrance to the forest, which is where the trouble usually happened, and when it did they packed the girls off to the nearest convent to wait it out, giving them a great scold – for how could they expect Madame la Comtesse to employ them up at the château if they are not respectable? The girls would reply that they didn't want to be employed up at the château, they wanted to go to Nagère and be secretaries. "That's not what you will be if you go to Nagère," Soeur Blanche would say.

Through the trees on the other side of the still, green river is the Château of Tourbonnière itself. It is basically unchanged today. Large grill gates open onto a tree-lined driveway that was very overgrown at this time.

In front of the house is a large flat piece of lawn around which the drive makes a circle. Moss and grasses had made it a little indeterminate. One wing of the house – the main part of the château which includes the main entrance – is to the left as one faces it. This left wing is more or less recent – that is to say it dates from 1725 – but on the right, the smaller stones, the uneven tiled gables and the glimpse of the old tower, show the original building to be historic.

Behind the building are the tall trees of the forest which rise up dark green against the grey skies of the north of France.

A somewhat low terrace leads into a front vestibule with a bare stone floor and walls studded with boar's heads; they are hung with riding crops and hunting horns of another generation. This, the newer part of the house, opens into the salon on the right, library to the left. Two generations earlier the downstairs windows had been filled with stained glass because an eccentric great-grandparent of the de la Rocque girls had made a hobby of stained glass images. He had filled the windows of his three homes with *des scènes gallantes* in carefully leaded colors. These illustrations of 18th century ladies and gentlemen in somewhat compromising attitudes, copied from artists such as Fragonard, have darkened the downstairs rooms ever since. Upstairs a first and second floor of bedrooms were musty and smelled of disuse; at the end of the first floor hallway was the W.C.

Tante Madeleine Marie, as the girls called their great-aunt, otherwise known in the neighborhood simply as Mme. la Comtesse, was a widow of a cousin of their father's, co-heir to Tourbonnière. She was also the sister of Madame de Lespinasse and had heard a great deal about the girls through their constant correspondence. She was equally hopeful of being helpful to them. She was very kindly disposed toward their father, who, on moving to America, had relinquished his rights to the old place. Her own heirs were nephews of her late husband's, who only came for the briefest of visits.

She was delicate, kindly and dressed in black; she was economical, soft spoken, pious and unworldly; in all these things she closely resembled her sister.

She was also thoughtful. Before her guests came – the cousins from America – she polished the little holy water basins inside their bedroom doors, had the mattresses turned and aired; she also put a little sign in the W.C. – "Please do not flush more than twice a day."

She wanted to make it pleasant for them – she planned to have soup before the main course at dinner; when alone she would only have had a boiled egg and biscuit.

The older part of the house had been declared a historic monument (her lawyer had insisted on that to save her from higher taxation), but they had not suggested opening the house to the public – there was no reason to do so. There was nothing to see; what was to be seen was the ancient tower to the rear of the building, which could be viewed best from one's car if one drove into the farm at the back.

Tourbonnière's happiest days had been 17th century ones when the manor was thriving and young men of the family went off to fight in Holland. Smallpox and a touch of what was thought to be a recurrence of plague, but may have been measles, had killed off most of the village a generation later. Subsequently, the family had been given richer lands in the centre of France and had not returned to Tourbonnière until after the Revolution.

On sunny mornings you could see ducks and chickens wandering in the lane leading to Tourbonnière. Madame de Lespinasse was always shocked by this and told her sister that it was deplorable to allow the farmer to be so careless; all the world's ills come from a lack of discipline; to this Tante Madeleine Marie would respond, "What can the farmer do? There is a hole in his fence and he says the price of wire is dreadfully high."

During the stay of the American cousins, she meant to make some pleasant evenings and had asked the village curé – the one at odds with Soeur Blanche – to leave his rectory on a few evenings and play some after-dinner games with her guests.

Tourbonnière has always had a storm-grey mood during the rainy summer days. The trees behind her toss and there is a haunted quality to the atmosphere – dark and romantic – and from within the library, sombre with the stained glass scenes of musketeers and décolleté ladies, there is a timelessness to her. On sunny days she seems to wait in an eternal pastoral day, waiting for well-born provincial ladies to come to draw and paint pale watercolors of the farm buildings, stone gateways and trees; this is what they used to do before the modern day.

There, on summer afternoons, there is also the sound of the not-too-distant electric plant, pumping electricity to village and château from the unequal flow of the green river – the enterprise of the priest and a neighboring retired colonel.

During the summer months Tante Madeleine Marie would play grandmother to a number of great-nephews and -nieces, at which time they would wander about somewhat aimlessly with a visiting Buisson Fleuri boy or an exchange student from England. They had no particular occupation while there, except for a much neglected intention to cram for a September exam. Occasionally the older ones would pile into the family car and go as far as the nearest similar country château to sit around with the young people there. There was timelessness to it, unbroken by the distant barking of dogs or the rare sound of a motor vehicle of some kind.

The day the American cousins were expected Tante Madeleine Marie went herself, wearing a hardy old apron over her longish black skirts, to open the gates. There was no knowing what time they might arrive. The train from Paris arrived at noon at Nagère, but there might be any amount of waiting for a taxi – not all taxis were willing to drive that far from the town; then the family might want luncheon in the station hotel, and it was quite a distance in any case. She spent the afternoon darning a tear in one of the lamp shades.

A gust of wind blew an odd shadow over the countryside. There would be rain. Today the villagers of Tourbonnière will still show you where the aristocrats were killed, but they will also tell you about the day the Americans came.

When they talk about the Americans they do not mean the cousins – the two young ladies and their parents who were family and belonged there, after all. They got quite used to them in a day or two – peering out of kitchen windows as the girls walked past, happening to be there when they could say good morning and see what they were wearing. The village argued nightly over which of the young ladies was the most beautiful. Soeur Blanche held that Francesca had more what she termed the face of the family. She said she had character and *je ne sais quoi* in her expression. She decided she was the image of her great-aunt Françoise, for whom she was named. Soeur Blanche was safe in saying this as she was the only one who remembered the great-aunt. Soeur Marie said that any idiot could see that the younger was *une belle*; none of the pictures you saw of the women of Paris were any more lovely than those features and she had an air about her.

The baker's wife said they were very Americanized, which brought down some Gallic scorn from her son, Gaston Grattecap, gardener and general handyman on the château grounds. He said that was absurd; they were typically French and if she had ever left the village to go any further than Nagère she would realize that. The trouble with Maman was that she thought she knew everything. Everyone knows that Americans are tall and thin and have huge mouths.

The second day of their stay, news had been brought to the village by the girl who worked in the kitchens that Mademoiselle Françoise (Francesca) was very helpful but that the younger sister jumped if the telephone rang, and always looked disappointed if it was not for her.

"If she is nervous it is the bad air of Paris that has done this to her," said the baker's wife.

"Typical," said her son the gardener, who once did a landscaping course in Le Mans, paid for by Madame la Comtesse. "Typical of someone who does not know the world." He crossed his legs and spread out a gnarled hand to point out the truth of his arguments on his fingers:

"A beautiful girl is nervous, why? *Eh bien*, as any fool knows, all young women have nerves nowadays. It is done above all in America – the nervous breakdown, the *crise de nerf.* There are, without any doubts, young millionaires in the picture." He had not thought of minor royalty.

You could tell that he, Gaston Grattecap, was the only one who had travelled; that they could not see that.

Mme. Mécontent, the village postmistress, sniffed. What did he know? She knew about the telephone. There was a man with a German name who had put a call through to their father. He said he would stop by on his way to Ruissy. That, in her opinion, was what made the mademoiselle jump. What did Gaston know? The man had the kind of name that, in her opinion, sounded like some kind of royalty.

She meant to keep this to herself, as she always denied that she listened to the telephone conversations that came through the post office, but it was a temptation that overwhelmed her. Why should Gaston think he knew everything?

So it is not the visit of *les deux Mademoiselles* that they will tell you about at Tourbonnière – after all, they were of the name – no, the day they don't forget was the day that a red Mercedes came through the woods into the village at four in the afternoon. It came at a speed that brought everyone to their front doors, or made them lean back from the ill-defined roadway. There were two young men in the car, which was an open one; they came to a stop, however, to ask Gaston Grattecap the direction to the château.

This was exactly the kind of young man, so thought Gaston, who was responsible for the young lady jumping when the telephone rang. He did not resent it, despite the fact that Mademoiselle, like all Tourbonnières, was the property of the village. It was the lot of the nobility to have things happen to them. He looked at the two young men appraisingly through eyes that were crinkled up and told them the way to the château gates. His assistant told him, as they drove on, that Madame liked tourists to look at the château and the old tower from the farm road at the back.

"Idiot! These are not tourists. It should be obvious even to a half-wit like yourself, that these are American millionaires – friends of *les Mademoiselles*."

Tante Madeleine Marie heard the car in the driveway. Nothing that bright a red had ever appeared in her driveway before. She was in her bedroom where she was cutting up newspaper into five inch squares for use in the W.C.. All her newspapers were religious ones and she always removed all religious symbols or references to His Holiness before she put the squares for use there.

She removed her apron now and went to the stairs. She told Chantal, the girl from the village, to stop standing there and go and tell *les Mademoiselles* and their mother that someone had arrived.

She would have preferred to leave it all to their father, but he had taken her vintage car into town to have something done to it.

Catherine also heard the car in the driveway; she hurried to the front door from her letter-writing hoping it was her husband. She was anxious for him as there had certainly been some very odd noises and smoke coming from the old car. Tante Madeleine Marie reached the front door first, making sure the combs in her hair were in place.

Clarky Finch stepped out of his Mercedes.

Clarkson Beard Finch is honest enough to admit that his arrival at Tourbonnière didn't turn out exactly as he had anticipated.

He and Alex, who felt responsible for introducing the Krazniks to the idea of Tourbonnière as a location, had arranged to go there at the same time. They had intended to be there early in the day, and, like the Krazniks, had planned to go on to Ruissy – taking advantage of having met the duchess.

They had gone so far as to fully explain to Sam Kraznik, who had only spoken on the telephone to the girl's father, that they would be glad to introduce them to the family. They also said that they had spoken to the duke and duchess, as a matter of fact, and they had said that the film crew was welcome to see the castle. They suggested that Sam could spend a couple of hours at each place and take a good look around.

Now, as Clarky stepped out of his Mercedes, he realized they had lost Tina and Sam on the road somewhere. Then there was something about the quiet overgrown solitude of the old place which, combined with the thought of seeing the girls, caused him a sudden attack of nerves, which rendered him more speechless than usual. Worse than that were the expressions on the faces of the four ladies who met him in the hallway, who seemed to be expecting someone else. Now it was past four and the Krazniks were nowhere to be seen.

"Hi there," said Clarky.

In the kitchen Chantal, the girl from the village, told the kitchen maid that Madame wanted tea served to the two young Americans who had just arrived. The kitchen maid dropped the jug she was holding: Imagine! Millionaires in the house and royalty on the telephone (the girl from the village knew all about the telephones at the central PTT office) – to say nothing of M. le Comte, as they addressed Xavier de la Rocque, himself here after so many years.

Francesca and Beatrice took Clarky and Alex into the old salon. Clarky and Alex were nervous. They felt in the way and were wondering what had happened to the Krazniks. The light would be gone soon and they were a long way from a town.

****

In fact, half an hour behind Alex and Clarky, Tina had told Sam that she wanted to fix herself up in the hotel in Nagère. Now they were being driven through the wooded region toward Tourbonnière in the studio car.

They were followed by Buddy Holzer in a Volkswagen beetle with a back seat loaded with cameras. Beside him was his special leather folder in which he had carefully put the prints and negatives of his pictures of Max, with the name and telephone number of his contact at the Kravonian embassy and that of their negotiator. He wanted to have a last talk about the situation with Tina – they had to move on this.

Behind the Volkswagen was the studio station wagon (everyone had a station wagon in those days) with the cameramen, who were telling yarns about locations they had known. They whipped out light meters and cameras as they passed the pale shafts of soft light that shot down between the tall trees. "J...... . C......... ! Get a load of that!" They were all poets in their way.

As the road grew narrower, it occurred to Sam that they might be lost, and, after all, they were getting late; he wanted directions. As it happened, by the time the Kraznik's Jaguar, Buddy's Volkswagen and the studio station wagon paused near the *Calvaire* to look at a map (people used maps in those days).

Gaston Grattecap, still working on the roadside, had taken on the character of village leader, guide and philosopher. As he explained to his assistant, a young fellow with one front tooth, "*Sapristi!* Any fool could see the difference between these people and the first two in the Mercedes. The first two were obviously young millionaires who would be calling on *les jeunes Mademoiselles*, whereas these were obviously not friends of *les nobles*, but were interested in the château. They must expect things like this now that Americans were coming.

Therefore when hailed by Sam and asked, "Oo ai ler chatto?" he leaned his elbow against the window of the Jaguar, tilted his beret the way he thought an official guide would do, and directed the motorcade toward the road that runs to the farm, from which a view of the old part of the château and its tower is obtained without disturbing the old lady.

After all, this afternoon Madame had guests, and the family had been called several times from Paris that day, according to the post-mistress.

Certainly the ivy-covered tower of the château is better appreciated from the farm. Photographers, as we have noted, were always directed that way. Unfortunately, the farm lane, by-passing the farm yard, ends in something like a pathway.

Normally, tourists step out of their car, take a few pictures, turn around, and leave again. Sam Kraznik's chauffeur, however, was looking for an entrance to the château itself, and could not have turned around anyway, being closely followed by Buddy Holzer and the studio station wagon.

The camermen in the studio car were discussing wide-angle lenses and hardly noticed the lurch and bumping of their car. The Jaguar moved on over softer and greener terrain until it stopped. It stopped because it was faced by a mud patch that gradually became a river, and also because its wheels were stuck. Above the patch of muddy green and the river an evening wind was rising. A Holstein's bell clanked as she came over to reconnoiter with these strangers.

There was the sound of the village church bell in Tourbonnière ringing for the five o'clock evening service.

Sam said, "God dammit, Steve, where is this? This is some kind of goddam farm. Geeeez."

Buddy Holzer put his head out of the sliding roof opening of his Volkswagen and smelled the air and said to himself, "Boy, but I bet they raise fine horses around here!" He could see the group of Holsteins in pastures of leisure, standing in the mud beneath the trees, and the end of a wooden bridge that didn't look as if it was used much. Behind them and to one side was the tall tower of Tourbonnière. Two rooks flew out.

The sky above was achieving the blue-black look of summer storms in the northwest, and the wind blew a little colder. Two of the cameramen in the station wagon got out with light meters and began getting their cameras into focus. Since the weaving of the great tapestries of the Low Countries, the lights of France have fascinated artists with its low blue hazes and blue green trees; these photographers felt just as they had.

The Jaguar continued to snarl and spin its wheels; the Krazniks looked around. Tina put her head out of the window and knocked her hat over one eye. She swore.

It took the farmer, a stout busy man, the station wagon and the horse-drawn farm wagon to extricate the Kraznik's Jaguar from the mud – and it took time. Tina stood outside the car, her white doeskin shoes becoming brown and smelling in an odd sort of way. She was getting cold and the dark clouds had started to pepper them with hard little raindrops.

The people in the château did not hear the sound of squealing motors and heaving men; they were having tea and *petit beurre* biscuits on the *petit point* chairs in Tante Madeleine Marie's salon – but the noise was heard in the village.

One by one the people came, starting with young boys and ending with Soeur Marie and Soeur Blanche on their motorized bicycles. The village curé joined them, rolling up the sleeves and tucking up the skirts of his cassock, to help them pull the farm horses forward with "Eeeeee!"

Gaston Grattecap, who came to watch, explained to his assistant that city people are not used to the country and will drive like that – straight into a river, if there is no sign to stop them.

Buddy Holzer, having lifted himself up onto the back of his car seat to poke his head through its sliding roof, got a good shot of Tina standing in the mud. You never knew what would come in useful. That was some kind of cruelty. It had begun to occur to Buddy that Sam might like the pictures of her with Maximilian as little as the people in Kravonia. If, he thought, Sam cut up rough when they came out it could well be the end of his marriage to Tina, so a few pictures like this might be useful.

But Buddy liked this place. He hadn't been to Normandy since he had been a young photographer with the invasion force. He would like to stay around for a while and get some pictures of villages he had known. The place brought back memories of quite another lifetime, when he had been young and in danger and part of something big. Seeing this countryside made him wonder what had happened to all that.

Meanwhile Xavier de la Rocque, having completed his errands in Nagère – a visit to the bank, and renting a dependable car, while leaving his aunt's venerable antique to be worked on, drove back toward the château. He had not visited these trees, this stretch of ground, this road, for some years. His trips back to France had been to Paris and they had been brief ones. He had been reluctant to visit Tourbonnière since relinquishing his share of it.

For a Frenchman, who no longer lives in France, there is a bittersweet sentiment attached to revisiting these places. Nostalgia is oddly mixed with relief that these acres are no longer any responsibility of his, with the endless battle over the taxes, or the subsidies and inheritance laws. At times like this the sense of loss outweighs the relief.

He was thinking something like this just as the rain began and he reached the part of the road which curves, giving a glimpse of a small lake beyond the trees where the building of the château comes into view. It was very French.

Whatever might have been his thoughts, they were interrupted by the puzzling sight of the red sports car in the château courtyard. His own arrival caused a confusion of welcomes: Chong Sam rolled on the floor and made noises like a clogged drain, his wife came forward with relief, and Tante Madeleine Marie exclaimed at the rented car. Alex and Clarky stood in the hallway under the stairs and felt forgotten. It was really raining at this point and they felt they ought to clear out, but where were the Krazniks?

They soon saw where the Krazniks were as the Jaguar, the station wagon and Buddy's Volkswagen came round from the farm, just as the rain began to sweep down. The two boys didn't know how they were going to handle all the introductions.

Kraznik and the cameramen left their cars and dodged the deluge into the entry of the château – there seemed to be a great many of them.

Tante Madeleine Marie turned to Xavier, just taking off his coat, "*Mais qui est qu'ils sont, tous ces gens*?" she exclaimed (for those who do not speak French: Who are all these people?) "*Mais qu'est qu'il se passe? Qui est ce qu'ils sont, ces gens*?" ("But what is going on? Who are they, these people?).

Sam Kraznik came into the foyer exasperated with it all, shaking the raindrops off his hat when he saw Xavier, "I'm Sam Kraznik," he said, "Would you be Mr. de la Rocque? We're kind of late. We meant to be here early in the day. We need pictures of the tower, you know, like we said."

Xavier's grey eyes twinkled at the absurdity of the scene, much as they had done at the Bilco Ball.

"Yes, we spoke in Paris on the telephone, but I had assumed you would be sending out an agent; this looks like quite a large crowd."

Sam, wet and disoriented, was glad to talk with someone who spoke English, and made sense.

"We're doing location shots," said Sam, "it takes a team. It looks like we won't get them tonight."

At that moment a crack of thunder shook the house; lightning flashed and torrents of rain swept through the *cour*.

Sam was not someone who liked to waste time or effort, but, in his way, he was also an artist. Despite his annoyance with the rain and the mud, he was able to see: first, this was, in fact, a very interesting location, and, second, that he could not look at the tower properly that evening.

He decided the best thing was for his team to get pictures of the interior of the old house in which they found themselves, and get the tower when they could.

He remarked to Xavier as his men came in taking off dropping jackets, "I'll tell you what – we better get some pictures now, while we can."

Not equipped to understand the French with which Xavier then tried to explain all this to his aunt, he said,

"Let's get the lights on, Steve. Let's light up the hall up there and those rooms down here."

"But they will make jump all the fuse!" cried Tante Madeleine Marie (*This is a rough translation of what she exclaimed*) – "The pump of the electricity has not work since three days."

She turned to her left where she saw Tina. Tina had taken her shoes off. Alex and Clarky, still standing under the carved wooden stair landing, felt it was just like at the Bilco Ball – they felt responsible for the situation and yet neither enjoyed it nor could they stop it. Clarky nodded at Tina with his Hi There smile.

The studio men were walking the length of the rooms downstairs, the rooms hung with boar's heads and portraits of ancestors displaying the Tourbonnière chin and eyes.

"Hey, Joe, get a load of these."

Francesca took charge of some of this. She asked the cameramen and Buddy to go with her into the kitchen where they could dry off and where there was room for them all in the pantry area.

Buddy looked appealingly at Tina, but she couldn't help. Her shoes were ruined and her hair was wet.

Lightning struck somewhere within the forest; the rain splashed down. It didn't look as if anyone was going to get away soon, although Alex and Clarky sensed it would be best to make themselves scarce. They had another concern, as Clarky said to Alex in an undervoice – if they were stopping by Ruissy, it would have to be next day and perhaps it would be better to make some arrangements about it. They didn't feel that arriving impromptu had worked very well in this instance.

Then as the blackest of the clouds broke and wind and rain swept through, they quietly slipped away together in the direction of the village in search of a telephone, and directions to a hotel in Nagère as well. They left just in time. The rain beat down on the stained glass windows in the library, it rustled in the ivy on the Tourbonnière tower, it pattered on the slate roofs of the old buildings. There were large puddles everywhere.

Tina sat alone in the drawing room with Chong Sam. The lights had all dimmed to a dull glow – something to do with the drain on the electricity. She sat and stared at a tapestry depicting huntsmen surprising a unicorn grazing. Chong Sam lay in the middle of the rug, his arms folded inwards Mandarin style. He looked at her balefully with an occasional glance at her white doeskin shoes lying on the floor beside her chair; he did not like Tina and was feeling neglected in any case. Tina blew her nose and wondered if he bit.

In fact, it had become obvious that no one could now get away at all. This was already obvious to Gaston Grattecap who was taking tea with Soeur Blanche and Soeur Marie, "They will have to stay the night, the fools, and what will Madame give them to eat?"

"But I will go – this is easy to arrange," exclaimed Soeur Blanche.

Meanwhile, the two de la Rocque sisters had gone to the kitchen; they felt they should prepare something for all these guests to eat. But what? Their father came and poked about in the wine cellar looking at the labels on his aunt's wine, while they all talked at once; Beatrice found some carrots and potatoes to peel.

It was then that Soeur Blanche arrived on her motorized bicycle wearing a black oilcloth tent she had made herself, modeled, it would seem, on a Ku Klux Klan pattern, and which protected her and her habit from all weather. She arrived, streaming water, with two chickens and a huge bunch of radishes.

She said she thought perhaps they would be needing extra fowl. She came in by the kitchen door, removed her Wellington boots, and put her basket down on the wooden kitchen table. She said she would make a *Poulet Breton* – Madame la Comtesse was not to worry herself. She was there to be of service.

Soeur Blanche had no intention of letting anything happen in the village, or in the château, that she had not organized to everyone's good.

Francesca and the girl from the village got out linen sheets smelling slightly of mould, and made up endless beds in rooms musty with disuse. She could hardly air the sheets with the rain pounding down – they would have to do.

The lights did not go out altogether, they only dimmed somewhat. The family sat down to a late dinner with Sam and Tina. The cameramen and Buddy stayed in the kitchen area which was, in fact, far more comfortable. In the dining room conversation was awkward and centered on the weather.

At ten o'clock Sam Kraznik was ready for bed. He stubbed out his cigar in the Holy Water receptacle beside the door and said he needed a shower. The main bedrooms were on the first bedroom floor, but the larger ones had already been allocated to the de la Rocque family, so he and Tina had been given a medium-sized room near the stairs that rose up to the next floor.

Their room backed onto the older part of the building from which the suspicious might imagine they heard the scratching and rustlings of mice, but the room itself was pleasant. The cameramen had been put up on the upper floor in what had once been servant's quarters – in the days when there were servants – and their feet could be heard on the bare floorboards above.

Sam's room was furnished with an Empire-period dressing table, five feet by three, with a marble top and a matching desk. There were two *papier maché* chairs and some multi-colored rugs on the floor.

Sam's feet were cold and he looked around for the door to the bathroom to take a shower. The door he opened was a closet, however, and a bit jammed. When it opened three bolsters and a small mattress came down on him, together with a print of the Virgin and Child by Foreggio. The other door showed him Buddy Holzer getting ready for bed. Sam decided there was no shower attached to his room.

Tina pointed out to him that in the corner of the room there was a basin. The small basin was within a small area curtained off by a cotton liberty print dating from 1905. Behind this curtain was a triangular stand for the basin and jug of water – water which had always been brought up by someone from the kitchen. At this time this was still the case and hot water would still have to be carried up from below. There had been no call for Tante Madeleine Marie to modernize the plumbing; she lived alone and it seemed to her to be an unnecessary and self indulgent expense.

Tina told Sam that he had to use the jug of water and the china bowl inside the curtain area, but neither of them could decide where to spit out toothpaste; they hesitated to open the shutters to spit outside with the rain still coming down. The shutters had been closed for the night by Chantal, who had also turned down the bed covers.

Sam sat down on the bed and pulled off his shoes. He and Tina had been given a double bed with a heavy Empire headboard carved out of mahogany; it rose to form the neck and head of a swan that reached over the sleepers.

A little later he set off down the hall in search of the bathroom. He wore Morocco leather mules and a colorful silk dressing gown. But he had lost his sense of direction in the hallway, which was paneled between the doorways, with an eighteen-inch red strip of carpeting running down into the darkness.

Tante Madeleine Marie was an acute hostess, however, and when she heard a hesitant creaking of the floorboards she appeared abruptly out of the shadow and said,

"Ah, *Monsieur,* you seek the little corner."

He returned some minutes later to say to his wife that if they ever got caught out staying with the nobility again, he was coming with torches and a plumber. He added that if they used this place as a location there were a helluva lot of changes he'd make around the place – the first being the installation of five tiled bathrooms with heating. He didn't sleep well.

Tina woke in the morning with a little gasp of fright. Where was she? Who was this beside her? Her back hurt. She stared ahead of her and saw a framed etching of The Vigil. The wall was a faded wallpaper in brown and pink stripes.

Slowly she got up – remembering. She was coming down with a bad cold and there was no curl in her hair – and she doubted if her hair-curler would plug into any outlet she could see. She fumbled with the shutters, which opened from the inside until they opened, and then she threw them wide. Below her lay the dewy view of overgrown gardens; grey blue smoke rose from the farm; young women were seen feeding chickens grain, and from the village came the ring, ring, ring of M. le Curé's little church bell.

Suddenly, Tina felt very sad.

The cameramen were already in the kitchen. They sat on the stone sink and wooden table eating bread and trying a few French words on Chantal. Chantal understood that they wanted eggs for breakfast (eggs for breakfast!! what an idea!) and began making them an *omelette.*

Francesca came downstairs and joined her mother and aunt putting out bowls for the *café au lait,* as well as bread and napkins the length of the dining room table. She came down early to try to help organize the unlikely crowd.

Beatrice quietly took her father's arm and drew him outside. She felt strange; she walked with him down the dewy avenue of trees and over the bridge and along the river, talking quietly about the person she would always think of as the man in the Ritz. For once in her life Beatrice had forgotten to bring out Chong Sam for his walk – he stared at them out of a window.

Gaston Grattecap, at work unusually early to make sure that the doings at the château did not go unappreciated, tweaked his beret at them and said, "*Messieurs/dames*."

Buddy Holzer was not at all sure of the morning procedures. He got dressed when he heard the voices of his fellow photographers outside and felt perhaps he could take the odd picture for the French tourist bureau in case anything came of the place as a location.

He unlocked his case that held his smaller camera and film. He thought he'd better try to collect on his negatives of Max and Tina soon, before the situation got too old; the people in Kravonia should have made a decision by now.

Sixteen kilometers to the west, the Duchesse de Ruissy found her husband in the round tower drawing room. The circular room was upholstered in silver and rose; on one side it commands a view of the sunken gardens – a moat in time gone by; on the other side was the river Esse.

Once, of course, the river had fed into the moat, and the moat had been crossed by a drawbridge protected by a portcullis. As one passes through the arched gateway into the great courtyard today, one can still see the mechanism by which the bridge had been raised anchored in the wall.

"*Chérie*," said Henriette: (translated) "Are you sure those movie people are going to arrive? I was convinced they were coming yesterday afternoon."

"I believe the young Americans left a message that they would be here today in the afternoon."

"But *Chérie*, it is possible that they would have spent the night on the way. Perhaps they are in Nagère. They could not stay at Tourbonnière, it is a ruin."

"We will see soon enough," said the duke, who was very resistant to the idea of trying to wrest a contract for a location from the old lady at Tourbonnière.

"And Maximilian said he was coming to Normandy, *Chérie*."

"My dear wife, if Maximilian is coming to Normandy it is not to look at castles, I assure you, and he would have every reason to visit the old place."

At Tourbonnière that morning the cameramen took pictures, and were served the *café au lait*. Sam brought suitcases downstairs. Francesca helped in the kitchen; their mother and father made the best conversation they could in order to take the burden from the old aunt.

Chong Sam watched. He had not been taken on the walk; he had not been spoken to even. Now, as he went toward the kitchen area to find his mistress and locate the smells, someone brushed past him and the door closed. Closed on his abbreviated nose.

Whoever closed the door on Chong Sam was not aware that he had closed it on a white Pekinese in whose veins ran the blood of Chi-Chu Yen and Ling Fi, a furry personage who had until that moment been sole owner of and protector of Her.

There was an odd expression in Chong Sam's two protuberant eyes – indignation quivered beneath quantities of white hair. Then he turned like an animated dust mop and flumped his way up the stairs. Chong Sam had put up with an awful lot – farm dogs in front of this house, the smell of mice in damp upstairs corners, Tina Kraznik's perfume (and he had resisted eating her shoes).

Well it was going to stop. He could have gone out with Her in the dewy morning for the walk. He could have wagged his tail impertinently at the village curs, eaten the long grass beside the river. He had been left behind and neglected. There had been no morning brush of his fur, no proper conversation. Now the door was shut on his nose and She had forgotten him! He, Chong Sam, son of a grand champion, perfect specimen of his kind. He quivered with rage.

He trotted along the upstairs corridor, snuffling under doors. One of the doors was open. Chantal from downstairs was making a bed. He went in. He wished it was Tina's so that he could get at those white doeskin shoes that smelled so good. He'd have rolled on them, chewed them, dragged one of them downstairs and growled over it – but there might be something in here.

Chong Sam was in Buddy Holzer's room. There didn't seem to be anything particularly attractive to him at first, but then he smelled leather. There was something leather! He dragged it down off a chair. Chantal was in the curtained area filling an empty jug with hot water. He threw her a wary look, dragged his find under the bed, gave it a good shake and then proceeded to chew.

The morning went by. Cameramen continued to take shots of the interior of the tower, which might interest Sam's director. Francesca went through the rooms and up the tower with the crew to show the way, to open windows, and warn them of the old mowing machines stored at its base.

Buddy took Tina on one side and said that he was pushing for a deal on his pictures to the man in the Embassy, as soon as possible. He would split with her fifty-fifty. He said it looked like it was the political activists in Kravonia that would be the best bet; he had been told that this was not a good time for a scandal to hit the royal family and they would probably pay well to keep the whole thing off the front pages. As soon as he got back to Paris he would see what they could get. He didn't like Maximilian – his jaw was still sore where he had hit him.

Tina was scared of getting involved in blackmail, but Buddy reassured her. He said that she ran no risks; he would handle it all. He said that he had spoken again with the fellow who had been shadowing Max, and the papers were eager to see the pictures as well; so, of course, were the contacts made with the parties in Max's embassy who were anxious to see them and had asked for details on Tina's career.

They went slowly up the stairs to his room.

From the window to the door – from under the bed to the fireplace – were strewn the results of Chong Sam's morning activities. From the rent and torn leather folder to the cracked and exposed film containers, everything was damp and somewhat eaten. Negatives, torn and unwound, littered the floor – pictures were ripped down the middle and damp. All were destroyed or partly digested.

Nothing was left of Buddy's prints or negatives.

From under the bed, and the leonine form of Chong Sam, came the sound of a sneeze, then he came out, swished his tail and stalked past them.

He felt much better.

Chapter 12

It was all over.

By mid-morning the Kraznik party was ready to move on. No one was sorry to see them go. Xavier de la Rocque was kindly and firm about getting them on their way. He encouraged those taking pictures in the tower and gave the Krazniks clear directions to Ruissy.

Gaston Grattecap, Soeur Blanche, Soeur Marie, the woman from the post office and the parish priest were not sorry to see them go either. These were not, in their view, the kind of people that Madame should be troubled with.

The cavalcade slowly took off, with Buddy Holzer following in his VW Beetle, down the narrow lane that wound past the *Calvaire*, draped in its telephone wires, toward the main road.

Buddy was a sad man. As he followed the studio station wagon he shook his head over the fortune, and perhaps fame, of which he had been deprived by a funny looking dog. He slumped over the steering wheel as the cars all edged slowly past a car coming towards them in the opposite direction.

Buddy hardly noticed the blue Citroën that paused on the far edge of the road to let them by – he hardly glanced at it; he certainly did not see that it was driven by Prince Maximilian of Hohen-Zeitfest, nor did Prince Maximilian notice him as they edged past and he continued on his way to Tourbonnière.

Although Buddy didn't see Max, he was thinking of him. He thought he would let the whole matter drop – there was nothing he could do; he was not going to call the First Secretary or speak with their negotiator. He would have to forget the whole damn thing.

And as the cars squeezed past each other Tina was looking down at her nails. She would have to take her chances with Sam. She told herself that she had never really liked the idea of blackmailing – it scared her.

Maximilian, meanwhile, wracked with anxiety, had continued to look hourly at the papers. When he got to Tourbonnière he was welcomed in feigned surprise by all, except in the case of Tante Madeleine Marie, who really was surprised. No one in the village, certainly not Gaston Grattecap, were in the least surprised.

Invited to stay, he made excuses to go into Nagère to use the telephones; he wanted to call his brother's office in Peltz. No, they had not had any further contact concerning pictures of any kind. It had been, they thought, a hoax, as they had said earlier. But Maximilian knew that there were, indeed, pictures and he couldn't sleep. He went so far as to try to tell the man he came to call Prof. Roc that he was sometimes pursued by the paparazzi, who would do anything to make a scandal – just in case the worst happened.

He waited, but nothing happened.

In Paris once more, he was convinced that not only Beatrice, but her family would welcome what used to be known as paying his addresses. Having officially met Beatrice at the I Love Paris Ball, and under the aegis of a duchess, this could be done in a way that was correct and would please everyone. This was a new departure for Max and he enjoyed it. He felt that this lovely girl made up for everything. He was not sure what he meant by "everything."

Maximilian was able to introduce his mother to Beatrice and her family, although he still he held his breath. He could not understand why the pictures had not surfaced, nor any further word of any kind. What could have happened?

There was no one to tell him.

Queen Helen arrived full of relief and wonder to be introduced to the de la Rocque family; she duly invited them all to Peltz for a week as her son asked her to do. The possibility of an engagement in the royal family leaked out and all the writers, who had been so happy to mock society with the story of what had come to be known as the Bilco Ball, now raced to be the first to give details of the engagement; even the Leftist press enthused over the story.

The question of the pictures haunted Maximilian for a long time, however – even for years. The event changed him in several ways: he became more helpful to Peter; he developed his idea for the automobile industry successfully; he was less abrupt with inferiors, and every now and then he would look up to the sky with real gratitude. In fact, Maximilian was humbled.

Magazines such as *Paris Match* and *Jour de France*, had prepared to use two or three pictures from the Homer's Hummers debacle in the centre pages of their next issues, mocking the modern manners of the young.

They still had not gone to press, however, when Queen Helen of Kravonia announced – through the palace in Peltz – that her younger son, Maximilian Rudolf Christian Edward Alexander, would marry Mlle. Beatrice de la Rocque Tourbonnière on the 3rd of September in Notre Dame Cathedral – at this point the editors changed their plans for their covers, also. One of them replaced a picture of a record high-jumper, taken at an international games event, with a picture of Prince Maximilian and Beatrice dancing; on the inside they placed a large blow-up of her face with the caption, "The smile that conquered a prince."

An article accompanied the pictures explaining how the prince had fallen in love at first sight when presented to Beatrice at the I Love Paris Ball. It went on to say in large black type, "*L'Amerique présente à l'Europe une deuxième princesse*" (America has given Europe yet a second princess.)

Appointments were made through the Embassy for Beatrice to have an official photograph taken; Queen Helen established herself with her ambassador and his lady to organize and indoctrinate her future daughter-in-law in her role, and the traditions of her new country.

Madame de Lespinasse's plate was full. Every denizen of her building knew that Queen Helen of Kravonia had entered and crossed the courtyard to go to her apartment on a formal call, immediately following the one to Beatrice's mother. She did this at Beatrice's request, a tactful and thoughtful gesture that reassured Queen Helen of the true graciousness of her future daughter-in-law. Mme. de Lespinasse was truly grateful that Providence had left her on earth long enough to make the the meeting of Beatrice and Maximilian possible – by using her to find a place for the family to stay during this crucial time – an anecdote about Providence that she loved to tell.

Seeing the royal visit from their window the older Buisson Fleuri boy said to his brother, "You see what the *sacré* dollar can do for you. Now our cousin becomes royalty."

To which his brother responded, had he not said that in America there was everything, even Princesses?

Tina was not divorced by Sam for two years after that summer, at which time he divorced her to return to his second wife. After this, Tina lived a precarious life between Las Vegas and Mexico – where she spent time following the bull fights – but we heard recently that she had been offered a part ownership in a modeling agency in Pasadena.

Oddly enough, the director of *By Kiss and By Kin* fell in love with the idea of the old, dusty tower and did, indeed, use its upper loft to film the salacious sex scene that caused such a stir.

Tante Madeleine Marie never saw the movie, which was a good thing. Those who did see the film could note in the credits, in small print, a mention of thanks to the de la Rocque Tourbonnière family for location shots – the rest of the movie was filmed at Ruissy. This required some ingenuity on the part of the director, as Ruissy, with its landscaped sunken garden, manicured lawns, and beautifully preserved interior, was not at all in keeping with the tower or the novel, but as Henriette pointed out – they change everything in the movies, and he made it work.

The duke did not have to sell Bellefontaine.

Tante Madeleine Marie was amazed to receive a handsome cheque from Kraznik's company negotiated for her by her nephew. If you go there now you will find two brand new bathrooms and the lights no longer dim. There is a new, wider carpet in the hallway, although it is still a red one, and she has an extra girl in to clean.

There is now the sign on the road illustrated with a little château, which means that it is now under the sheltering care of the Society for the Preservation of Historic Monuments.

They finally cleared away the telephone wires which had draped the roadside *Calvaire* and improved the road to the château, although someone touched up the paint on the holy statues in much too garish colors.

Soeur Blanche and Soeur Marie try to stop Gaston Grattecap from taking credit for all the happenings at Tourbonnière, including the engagement of Mademoiselle Beatrice and the German Prince (as they insist on calling him.) They are not sure how they feel about his being German, but his manners and perfect French accent ended by winning them over. One must forgive, after all.

Buddy Holzer went on assignment to Peru to take location shots for a movie called *Golden Conquest*. He sometimes thinks about the fortune he lost because of a grumpy Pekinese. But as time goes by he thinks more about Normandy, its beauty and the old world charm he saw at Tourbonnière – to its suitability for horse raising, and to his youthful experience with the army and the Normandy Landings. He decided to frame some of the pictures he still had in a trunk.

When he sees pictures of Princess Beatrice or Prince Maximilian of Hohen-Zeitfest he shrugs with a rueful smile. The guy was in his hands for a while. There were winners and losers.

The First Secretary at the Kravonian embassy in Paris fulfills his duties punctiliously toward Princess Beatrice, although he remains somewhat jaundiced when he has to deal with the prince.

As already mentioned, Queen Helen and the Dowager Duchesse de Ruissy explain the meeting of Beatrice and Maximilian to their friends over coffee. Queen Helen says that men like Maximilian end by settling down and usually make the best husbands – that when strong men have sown their wild oats they revert to their parents' way of life. The Dowager Duchess agrees with this philosophy, while her daughter-in-law, Henriette, takes full credit for the couple having met.

Charlotte Schlemmer and her husband, Carl, now own a jewel of a small manor near Chantilly. Her luncheons are attended by everyone. She hopes one day to include TRH Prince Maximilian and Beatrice of Hohen-Zeitfest among her guests. In answer to invitations she receives very kind responses from the Princess's secretary explaining their very brief time in Paris and how difficult it always was to arrange anything informal.

Charlotte is still depending on the younger duchess to facilitate this for her one day.

Some time later there were some awkward questions asked about the source of the Ben Fazy fortune – with serious hints of arms trafficking. He was not officially accused of any wrong-doing, but he lost his somewhat precarious position in society and spent most of his time in Cairo after that. The Hôtel Plessis was put up for sale and bought by a German financier.

As time went by, Harry Alastair and Hugo Davenant both became executives in a firm of financial advisors in the City. They did very well and could be seen each morning in bowlers (young men still wore bowlers in those days), suit and tie, and reading the Financial Times in the train up from the country. They hunted on weekends. (Hunting was still allowed in England at that time). They both have sons at Eton.

Robert Robertson had a few hit songs and then went into real estate – his father-in-law being a successful developer in the north of England. You can see him sometimes as a judge on talent shows.

Alex Feldenstein is heard at gallery openings, snapping his fingers for more champagne and speaking of Beatrice; he corrects himself – Her Royal Highness Princess Beatrice, of course, a great friend of his.

On a sadder note:

In the south of France, somewhere on the hot, pine-perfumed Route Nationale #7, Ivan Nevsky, with Olivia Bryce-Smith beside him, took a bend too generously on one of those abrupt curves on the approach to Fréjus. Facing them, as they rounded the curve, was a five-ton truck and a Ferrari, taking it blind.

Ivan swerved violently and braked too hard; the car he was driving – borrowed from Alex – swung over, went out of control, and flew out into the ravine. It arched up and over – so slowly – before dropping directly down into the sand, rocks and conifers below. It slipped, twisted and crumpled up on its side – wedged between a rock and a fallen pine.

Fortunately, it was an open car and seat belts weren't worn then as they are today, which was, in this case, a good thing. The two of them were thrown free before the car landed, and although they were both very badly hurt, they both lived. Ivan would wear a back brace for years; Olivia was in coma for some weeks in a French hospital.

Mrs. Payne Glenn was truly shocked when she was told about her son's accident; she immediately called her lawyers and her business manager and commissioned them to see to it that he be flown to New York and put in the care of the top specialists in back surgery.

John Trent and Pauly were quietly very glad that they had not said anything too damning about the Bilco Ball when they they heard about the royal engagement. They were able to say – many times through the years – how they sensed something special about Beatrice when they met her in Paris, "long before she became known." And John liked to say, "I said to Pauly, I really did, no, *really* – I said when we first saw her in Paris, you could see she had a very special way about her – you could almost tell she was royalty, even then – and then at the Ball! Well, I mean, it was *obvious.*"

On their return to the United States Mr. and Mrs. Schlatz decided to spend time in their Texas home where the golf and tennis at the local Country Club was friendly and familiar. Patty did not wait to enroll in the University of Texas as they suggested; she eloped with the tennis instructor and is living in Austin. The young man says he does not want to work for Bilco and is happier on the tennis court. This story has not reached its final chapter.

We ran three pages of pictures of the wedding in our magazine: shots of the bride and groom leaving Notre Dame Cathedral, nicely framed against the gothic doors; another excellent shot of them in the open Rolls that took them back to the Embassy for the reception where, sadly, photographers were not allowed. Her wedding dress came from Calamagni.

Smaller marginal pictures showed the bride's parents speaking with King Peter and his wife and children. These were official pictures given to us by the office in Peltz, however.

Beatrice's parents were not at all altered by the celebrity that surrounded their younger daughter. Catherine continued to work with her favorite charities, and Xavier continued to give courses in international finance. At the Business School they still called him Prof. Roc, and his grey eyes continued to crinkle at the corners, as all of this had appealed to his sense of humour.

On her return to New York, following the visit to Peltz, the festivities that surrounded her sister's engagement and wedding, Francesca changed her mind about entering law school. She decided instead on a graduate degree in European History and Political Science. Shortly thereafter she had a phone call from Boston, where Olivier de Ruissy had arrived to continue his studies at MIT. He suggested coming to New York and seeing the family. Those of us in the press watched this with something like anticipation – another great story, which perhaps you remember.

Chong Sam, for his part, was not altogether happy in Kravonia, where he spent the remainder of his lifespan. He lived luxuriously, but he was walked by equerries and fed by servants. He saw less of Beatrice and had to share her with someone he was not at all sure he liked. But the gardens surrounding the smaller palace in Peltz were beautiful, and he felt they were worthy of his attention.

None of what I have told here was featured in my *Where Are They Now?* column, nor have I told how I came to know all this. And I will not tell you now.

In New York, Clarky Finch, home for the winter, stood on one leg on 57th St., near the Plaza Hotel. He had met up with Alex Feldenstein, back in the city for a winter exhibition.

Alex said,

"Adela Carr's in town."

www.ingramcontent.com/pod-product-compliance
Lightning Source LLC
Chambersburg PA
CBHW070544310726
48982CB00010B/1469/J
* 9 7 8 1 6 8 0 5 3 8 6 2 5 *